Enjoy!

SPIDER'S BIG CATCH

SPIDER'S BIG CATCH

More Tales From The Heartland

Gary E. Anderson

Writers Club Press
San Jose New York Lincoln Shanghai

Spider's Big Catch
More Tales From The Heartland

All Rights Reserved © 2002 by Gary E. Anderson

No part of this book may be reproduced or transmitted in any form or by any means, graphic, electronic, or mechanical, including photocopying, recording, taping, or by any information storage retrieval system, without the permission in writing from the publisher.

Writers Club Press
an imprint of iUniverse, Inc.

For information address:
iUniverse, Inc.
5220 S. 16th St., Suite 200
Lincoln, NE 68512
www.iuniverse.com

All characters and situations contained in this book are purely fictional, except for those characters and situations which are totally real and completely true. The trouble is, I can't remember which is which, so I'd appreciate if you didn't ask. It won't solve anything, and will only make me even more confused.

Beware: this book will cause both laughter AND tears!

ISBN: 0-595-23443-7

Printed in the United States of America

To my loving parents, who didn't laugh (in front of me, anyway) when I told them I wanted to be a writer and musician when I grew up, and to all those people in my life, including one very special woman, who helped me discover the truth about how human beings should act, think, and feel, even when the entire world seems to be spinning out of control. You taught me that no one is perfect. The trick is to keep trying…and to share some laughter and tears along the way.

Nothing, I think, so inadequate as language: to express in words not made by oneself concepts clear only to oneself. Words worn threadbare, sizes too small! How to stop a winged idea long enough to express it? Poor, inarticulate man.

> David Grayson, *Under My Elm*

Contents

Foreword xi
You Want It When? 1
Casey Rose's First Test. 3
I Can't Weight—One Man's Diet. 7
One Brave Rooster 11
Spider's Big Catch 15
June Weddings 19
Spelunking With Scooter 23
Quality Time? 27
The Bonfire. 29
A Stitch In Time. 33
Notes On Perfection 39
Need Some Help Cowboy? 43
Dad's Fishin' Pole 49
Take A Hike!. 53
Opal's China. 57
The Striped Cardinal 61
Some Thoughts on Email 65
Batter Up! 67
Lessons From Zen 71
Amazing Stuff. 75
Bob's Hook Shot 77

What's In A Name? 79
The Black Hole. 81
The Entrepreneurs. 85
My Year As A Tackling Dummy. 89
Opal's Cheater's Quilt 97
Quantum Fishin' 101
More Amazing Stuff 105
The Cold (Tablet) War 109
Small Towns—Not Small People 113
Family Pirate Stories 117
One For The Road—A Volleyball Trip 121
The Ramblin' Gary Show 127
Small-time Halftimes Are Big-time By Me 131
Old Dogs Dye Hard 133
Grandpa's Knife 141
About the Author *145*

Foreword

We were originally going to call this book *You Still Don't Get It, Mr. Anderson,* in honor of a piece of "fan mail" we got one day at *Iowa REC News,* which has featured my column, "Wit and Wisdom," on its back page every month 1996.

It seems we had made a grave error one month in a story called "Opal's Cheater's Quilt," which you'll find in this book. We got many wonderful pieces of mail about it, but it seems as if we had inadvertently put an "O" in place of an "I," turning the word "in" to the word "on." Not being quilters, it seemed like a small mistake to us, but apparently when you're actually making a quilt, stitching "in" is *very* different from stitching "on." There was no doubt that this lady was a serious quilter, and to her, we had committed a cardinal sin—so she let us have it with both barrels.

But it was her opening sentence that most caught my imagination. The lady began her letter by saying, "You still don't get it, Mr. Anderson…" and went on to let anyone who was interested know exactly what the difference is between "in" and "on" when it comes to making quilts.

Editor Bob Dickelman and his wonderful assistant, Ruth Rasmussen (whose name I promised to spell correctly in this book, since it had been misspelled in my previous one) quickly sent off a conciliatory letter, telling this avid quilter about the inadvertent typographical error. Then, just to be safe, they asked me if I would also write and apologize. I was happy to do it, partly because that sweet lady had been so passionate about her craft, and partly because her opening line had been running through my head, again and again, like a tape loop. ("You still don't get it, Mr. Anderson…You still don't get it, Mr. Anderson…")

After apologizing for the error, I addressed the other part of her letter. I told her that, in all honesty, she was absolutely right. I still don't get it. In fact, I am most happy to admit that I *don't* get it, I never have gotten it, and it's entirely possible that I never will. But to my mind, that's the whole point. I don't get it—and I know it. What's more, I told her, if I ever *do* get it, I'm out of a job. After all, my particular brand of humor is largely based on being totally confused, and it gives me never-ending fodder for material.

We never heard from her again, so either that passionate quilter accepted my apology or gave up on me as a hopeless cause. Being an inveterate optimist, I'm hoping it was the former.

But her point is well taken. If you talk to veteran writers, they'll generally give you some sound advice: write about what you know. I took that advice to heart when I first heard it, and it's worked very well for me over the years. Therefore, while writing about what I know, I spend a lot of time writing about being lost and confused. For instance, in my first book, *Spider's Night On The Boom*, there are at least three stories about being lost, and at least that many about being confused. Since I'm still writing about what I know, you'll find that to be the case in this book, too. They're subjects I know well, so I keep returning to them again and again.

A while back, one of Iowa's larger newspapers sent a reporter out to my little farm to check on my progress as a writer. The story ran in the Saturday edition, and I must admit, it was nice to have my fifteen minutes of fame. But then something unexpected happened. A friend of mine in California wanted to know where she could find a copy of that story for some research she was doing for her own story about me. I told her the newspaper archived their stories on the

World Wide Web, and that I'd look the story up and let her know where to find it.

So I visited the paper's website, and typed in "Gary Anderson." Needless to say, several articles came up, since Gary Anderson isn't exactly an uncommon name (there's a story about that in this book, too). But one unusual headline caught my eye, and I was delighted to find that story turned out to be about me.

The headline read, "Gary Anderson breaks out of confinement."

How I loved that little scrap of a headline! I nearly laughed myself silly. Even though they were only the first few words of a longer title, "Gary Anderson breaks out of confinement in big cities to find a home in rural Iowa," it seemed like such a perfect headline for an article about a humor writer. My very own blooper! I've laughed about that incident ever since, and as a storyteller, I've gotten a lot of mileage out of that headline since I first discovered it.

Over the years, I've gathered a number of stories like that, all brought about because somebody somewhere read my words, and it's a bit overwhelming at times, to tell the truth. After all, a writer never really knows if anybody is reading his words at all, much less being touched enough by them to sit down and write a letter…even if that letter does begin with, "You still don't get it, Mr. Anderson."

❦   ❦   ❦

As orders for autographed copies of my first book, *Spider's Night On The Boom*, began to come in, I was delighted to discover that 99% of those orders also included a personal note. (Some folks even sent cards. It was very sweet.) That almost meant more to me than the orders themselves, because it meant that my words were not only being read, but were touching people's lives in a real way, whether through their heart strings or their funny bones.

After all, writing isn't exactly a spectator sport. You sit in your studio, tapping on your keyboard and if you do it long enough, eventually you have an article. Then, if you tap out enough articles, eventually you have a book. But it's a solitary profession. In fact, I'd be hard-pressed to think of a writer who was able to create their best stuff in the midst of a crowd. By its very nature, writing must be done in private.

It's not like being a musician, where your audience applauds the instant you've finished your song. (I know. I was a professional musician for many years.) But it doesn't happen that way for a writer. You get checks from editors, which is nice, but it's only through "fan mail" and other feedback from readers that a writer knows if he's really touching them or not. So when folks take the time to sit down and add a note about a particular story or an idea that meant something to them, that means a great deal.

The notes varied considerably, from the touching to the comical. One lady said she gives speeches on a regular basis, and she just wanted me to know how often something she'd read in my "Wit and Wisdom" column in *Iowa REC News* over the years had given her an idea for a speech. When I autographed her book, I told her the ideas were hers to use, but to remember me as one of her best sources of material if she ever got famous and/or rich.

Another sweet lady sent me several wonderful memories from her own childhood, which, I must admit, put me in a bit of a spot, since my first thought was, "Wow! This is a great story. I bet I could rework this and use it in my column."

But after some soul-searching, I decided to stuff that lady's story into the tote bag of my mind, knowing that once enough time had gone by, the idea would resurface in a slightly different form, and by that time I wouldn't be able to remember whether it had happened to me, or whether I'd just heard about it. At that point, of course, it would be fair game…

Other readers ordered books to give as gifts for friends and relatives, which was also a sincere compliment. To me, it meant those folks considered my words valuable enough to want to share them with someone they cared about. That was a good feeling, too. One lady ordered two, saying, "I don't even know who I'm going to give this to, but I couldn't resist having an extra one on hand."

I'll tell you, that second copy was a hard book to autograph! Since I had no idea who would ultimately receive it, I couldn't put an actual name on it. But after some thought, I figured out a way around that dilemma.

I wrote, "If you're getting this book, I know something about you. I know that you must be a very special person, because Mrs. Jones thinks enough of you to want to give you this book as her special gift to you. I hope you realize that, and will thank her for her *real* gift to you…her love and respect."

That simple autograph gave me a chance to touch another person's life in a way I might never have been able to do on my own, since it's entirely possible that person had never read any of my columns or books. The gift Mrs. Jones gave me by wanting to give my book as a gift made *me* feel special, as well, and I won't soon forget that feeling. As a writer, it was the equivalent of applause, and I'm grateful.

I hope *you* enjoy these tales of the Midwest, be they silly or sublime, and whether you're a Midwesterner or not, I hope you see reflections of yourself, your friends and families among the stories contained in these pages. And when you find yourself looking squarely into that reflection, don't forget to smile…because from where I sit, you look *good*!

You Want It When?

One thing I've learned over the years: it doesn't matter whether you're a 10-year-old moving into a new neighborhood, or an adult entering a new workplace, there's one thing that will always remain constant. If you're the new kid on the block, you'd better make sure you're familiar with the territory before you start throwing your weight around. Everyone has had to face the situation of being the "new person" at some time in their lives, but one of my own such moments of truth came a few years ago, when I was hired as editor of a monthly magazine published by a large Midwestern church.

I was very excited about my new position, but it didn't take long for my excitement to turn to frustration. Shortly after I took over the reins, I began having difficulty adjusting to the leisurely pace of the magazine's staff members.

Don't get me wrong: it wasn't that the work didn't get done; it just never seemed to get done in what I considered a timely manner. From my previous experience as a newspaperman, I was used to a much stricter production schedule, and the relaxed atmosphere I encountered at my new post began to get on my nerves.

Month after month, I began to grow more irritable until one morning the situation finally came to a head. An important task I'd assigned a few days earlier hadn't been completed according to the schedule I'd outlined. It was the last straw, and I blew up.

I stormed into my secretary's office, blustering loudly about the complete inefficiency of everyone on the staff, from the writers to the production crew, and anyone else who might be related to the magazine in even the remotest fashion.

"Why hasn't this been finished?" I roared, pacing back and forth in front of her desk. "I'm not going to stand for this any more. From now on, I want assignments completed on time! I want a memo sent to every single person in this organization, stating in no uncertain terms that when I say I want something done ASAP, I mean I want it *done* ASAP!"

My secretary was a lovely lady who'd been with the magazine since its inception (which, if my information was correct, was shortly after Noah had finished unloading the animals...and his printing equipment).

She waited until I'd finally yelled myself out, then looked me squarely in the eyes, smiled demurely and said softly, "I'm sorry, sir, but I think you and the staff are simply having a bit of a communication problem. You see, you can tell everyone you want things done ASAP, and that's fine. But when you say that, you have to understand that around here, ASAP has always meant 'Any Sunday After Pentecost.'"

I wish I had a clever way to sum up how that lady's sweet words made me feel, but I don't. All I can say is that things began running much more smoothly from that moment on. As for who made the biggest change, I think I'll leave that to *your* imagination.

Casey Rose's First Test

When my kids were small, I made a vow not to become one of those parents who lived their lives vicariously through their children. And I did fairly well, too, until my firstborn, Casey Rose, entered kindergarten.

And even then I did pretty well, trying hard to let my daughter progress at her own pace, though I must admit to keeping a running total of the number of "smiley faces" at the top of the papers she brought home every day. In fact, it gave me great pleasure to see my child bringing home straight "smiley faces"…as good as it could get at that school.

Who knows, I remember thinking, we just might have a future Nobel Prize winner in our household! After all, I was willing to bet that even Albert Einstein hadn't brought bring home straight "smiley faces" when he was my daughter's age, and look where he ended up! It staggered the imagination!

Then one day, my daughter got off the school bus and came running up the driveway, holding out a sheet of yellow paper. Since she usually kept all her school papers in her backpack, I knew this one had to be something special. She stuffed the paper into my hand, and I read it as we held hands and walked back to the house.

The paper read, "In two weeks, we'll be doing special testing at the school. Please make certain your child gets a good night's rest the night before the test."

Whoa! That sounded serious. I began to worry about how my daughter was going to do. This was to be her first big test, and the paper had offered no instructions on how I could help my child prepare for it. It made me nervous, so I decided I'd better have a chat with Casey Rose's teacher.

The next day, I met Casey Rose at the school in the afternoon, before she got on the bus. Her teacher, Mrs. Kurth, was standing at the front door, and I asked if she had time to talk. She agreed and led us back to her classroom.

Back in her room, Mrs. Kurth, a short, stout lady with a wonderful smile and gentle voice, asked me have a seat. Looking around, I saw nothing but miniature chairs and tables, but finally managed to settle myself down onto a doll-sized chair (no mean feat for a guy 6'2"). I poured out my concerns about the test and how the note Casey Rose had brought home made the whole thing sound so important and serious.

I finished my questioning with, "I guess what I'm asking is: what can I do to help my daughter prepare for this test?"

Throughout my rambling, Mrs. Kurth just sat quietly, a patient smile on her face, waiting for me to finish. Then, without a moment's hesitation, she replied, "Give her a hug."

Although she'd said it quietly, the words struck me like a thunderbolt. I suddenly realized I HAD been making too much out of a kindergarten test and without thinking, I'd violated the vow I'd made to myself so long ago about not pushing my kids as hard as many of my friends were pushing theirs.

But I got the point. I smiled, thanked Mrs. Kurth, struggled to my feet, scooped my precious daughter into my arms, and walked out of the room.

Since that day, there's no doubt that my daughter has had to face many challenges in her life. But every time I've watched her approach one of those life tests we all must face, her kindergarten teacher's words come back to me, reminding me that sometimes there are situations in which the best thing we can do for our children is simply to give them a hug.

Thanks Mrs. Kurth…I got it!

I Can't Weight—One Man's Diet

Like many people, I've decided I need to take off a little weight from the holidays—the holidays of six years ago. But I've never dieted before, so being a conscientious kinda guy, I logged into my favorite web browser to look for some advice.

I found 3,978,158,342 sites offering help with losing a few pounds. (In fact, the number was so overwhelming that I had to go grab a sandwich before even *thinking* about tackling the search.) Now, as a public service, I'm going to try to encapsulate what I learned, although I must admit that I might have gotten a little confused by some of the terminology.

The first thing I noticed was that it seemed as if most of the sites I visited spent a considerable amount of time talking about calories, so maybe we should start there. I may be wrong, but as far as I could make out, a calorie is defined as the amount of heat it takes to raise a gram of water from 58 degrees to 60 degrees Fahrenheit.

Reading that definition immediately brought several questions to mind. First, how were those particular numbers chosen? Who made that decision? And why did they choose 58 and 60 degrees? I mean, that's not even hot enough to take a bath in!

Next, if one calorie raises the temperature of water two degrees, and the human body is 90% water, I couldn't help wondering why millions of Americans don't boil over during the holidays after consuming billions of calories at one sitting. It made no sense to me, and got my mind to wondering…

That definition of a calorie implies that a person should be able to eat a million calories a day, as long as they spaced them out, since the main concern would be simply to avoid boiling over. Using that logic, a person could eat a sizeable amount of anything they wanted, and then, as long as they let the body cool back down, they could eat a whole bunch more. Using that system, as long as you continued to monitor your body temperature and stayed below the boiling point, you'd never gain any weight! I admit, I may be missing the point, but it seemed to make sense to me.

What's more, unless I'm wrong, that concept must be pretty well understood by most of the world at large, which would explain why you so rarely see people boiling over in public. If you already knew that, I apologize, but like I said, I'm new to this dieting business, so the whole concept came as exciting news to me.

It was also kind of exciting to discover how a simple thing like learning how calories are measured could make so many other things I'd always wondered about fall into place. For instance, based on that knowledge, I found that I could suddenly offer an explanation for one of the strangest mysteries that has affected human beings over the centuries—spontaneous combustion. Using my "boiling over" theory, I was convinced that if investigators would only examine the area next to the easy chair where an unfortunate victim had burst into flames, they'd most likely find a half-eaten chocolate éclair or cream-filled doughnut. There's little doubt that last rush of calories was probably just enough to send that poor person's body over the boiling point. The end result? A whiff of smoke, a flash of fire…then a pile of ash and a half-eaten bear claw.

Based on my research, I've developed my own diet plan, and I'll be happy to pass it on to you. I call it my "Don't Boil Over" diet. Here's how it works: you can eat all you want, in as large of portions as you want, just as long as you don't consume enough calories to push your body temperature above 212 degrees Fahrenheit. It's that simple.

Oh, and another thing: be careful not to drink too much hot stuff while you're stuffing yourself, since you never know when you might push yourself over the edge. And by all means…if you smell smoke, back off!

Well, there you have it. Pretty simple, huh? But isn't that the way most great ideas are, if you think about it? Feel free to pass the diet plan on to your friends, especially anyone you might know who has looked as if they might be smoldering from time to time. Who knows? By sharing this information, you just might be saving them the embarrassment of bursting into flames at the next church potluck!

One Brave Rooster

It's funny, the things we remember from our childhood. Often the things we recall aren't those big moments we thought we'd never forget as those events were unfolding. More often, the things we remember are small, and totally unexpected. For instance, one of my own fondest memories is of a Sunday, an old rooster…and an amazing act of courage.

As a kid, it was my job to go out to the chicken house on Sunday afternoons and snare a hen for supper. I was never crazy about having to do it, but in those days, there was no debate when a mother or father told a kid to do something…you just did it.

So every Sunday afternoon, I'd walk into the chicken house and reach for the "chicken catcher" which hung on a nail just inside the door. Our chicken catcher wasn't "store bought." It was actually just a coat hanger that had been straightened out and then bent at a severe angle at the end, thus forming a hook.

The concept was pretty simple. All I had to do was swing the chicken catcher, hook a chicken by the legs and scoop her up. Since we always kept 30 or 40 chickens on our little farm, it was a fairly easy task to walk into the midst of the hens, blindly swinging the chicken catcher back and forth until I hooked one. Although it was a dusty job and got pretty noisy as the chickens raced to get out of the way, the whole process usually took only a few minutes.

But one day, my dad gave me a more challenging task. I was supposed to catch one specific chicken—a mean old rooster who'd begun to torment the other animals on the farm. (And I knew from painful experience that harassment also included any kid who was unfortunate enough to be walking across the barnyard when the rooster was in a bad mood—which was most of the time.)

So that Sunday, I was charged with a daunting task: not only did I have to hook the leg of one specific chicken among all those in the hen house, but that leg happened to belong to the meanest chicken I'd ever known!

Although I usually strode into the chicken house with confidence, that Sunday, I gingerly poked my head inside the door and carefully reached for the chicken catcher. Since they'd seen me perform this ritual many times in the past, the leghorns and barred rocks began to grow restless, each one knowing that this day could be their last.

My eyes scanned the feathered throng, searching for my intended victim. I found him milling against a far wall, unconcerned with my presence. He'd seen this routine many times, too, and his experience told him that it was always a female who finally disappeared at the end of all the confusion, so he didn't even give me a second look.

I carefully closed all the doors, my eyes locked on the rooster. The air was heavy on that hot summer day and dust began to rise as the chickens shuffled around, trying to stay out of my reach. I slowly worked my way through the crowd, constantly focused on my multicolored prey.

As I drew closer, the old rooster looked surprised as it began to dawn on him that I was singling him out. He gave me a questioning look, and even though he knew there'd obviously been some kind of mistake, he quickly decided that he probably should start taking some evasive action, and began trying to lose himself among the hens.

But I continued to pursue my quarry, taking occasional swipes at him with my chicken catcher whenever I could get close enough. I began to cough as huge clouds of dust and feathers began choke my lungs while frightened chickens scattered in every direction.

In the midst of the confusion, that old rooster and I played out our deadly game. I lunged. He ducked. I dived. He swerved. After a half hour of chasing that old rooster, my t-shirt was drenched and my face was streaked with a mixture of sweat and dust. But I was no closer to catching him than I'd been when I first walked in the door. (Many years later, I watched a funny scene in one of the "Rocky" movies in which his manager tried to increase his reflexes by having him chase chickens. I laughed at that scene, in large part because I'd been blessed with a special understanding of how hard chasing chickens can really be.) But this wasn't funny at the moment. It was hot, frustrating, and tiresome.

After a half hour or so, a change suddenly seemed to come over that rooster. He stopped running away and stood for a moment against the far wall, looking me straight in the eye. I was startled and stopped in my tracks, stunned by his new boldness. Before I could think, that rooster flew straight at my face, claws outstretched, murder in his eyes. In self-defense, I covered my face with my arm and flung the chicken catcher out in front of me. To my amazement, my hook caught the angry rooster by the leg, and he hung from the end of my chicken catcher, wildly flapping his wings and squawking in rage.

All other details of that long ago Sunday escape me now. I'm sure the old rooster was dispatched and became supper that night, although I also imagine he was as tough as shoe leather. But none of that has anything to do with what I remember now. Although the incident took place more than thirty years ago, the only thing I recall today is the bravery that old rooster showed in the face of his final hour. It had come down to either him or me, and he knew it. So, in spite of the odds, he took his best shot…and earned his rightful place in our family's history.

Spider's Big Catch

When I was in college, Spider McGee, Quick Charlie Fox and I loved to fish off the log boom in the river near my house on summer afternoons. We'd sit and talk about life, drink hot chocolate, and occasionally catch a fish or two. All summer long, one fishing trip was pretty much like any other, but one day, Spider yelled, "Hey, I got something, and it feels big!"

In our circle, catching any fish was always a pleasant surprise, but hooking something *big* was reason for genuine excitement. As Spider reeled, his straining pole was bent almost in half. He wasn't kidding—this was something big.

"This thing is a monster," he said, the drag on his reel screaming. Sweat began pouring down his forehead as he struggled against whatever had taken hold of his bait. After an hour or so, Spider had finally gotten his catch close enough to the boom for us to get a glimpse of it. But when we saw it, we couldn't believe our eyes.

It was a snapping turtle.

"Oh, man, that's too bad," said Charlie. "I thought maybe you'd hooked Old Granddad there, for a second. You better just cut the line and let him go."

"Are you crazy?" said Spider. "That's the lure my grandfather gave to my dad on his tenth birthday. It was hand-carved in Norway. He doesn't even know I have it! My dad'll kill me if I lose it. I gotta get it back."

"Well, how're you gonna do that?" I asked. It didn't take long before I was sorry I had.

"Well, I'll just drag the thing up to the edge of the boom, then you reach out and grab the lure out of his mouth," Spider said calmly, as if what he had just said wasn't the most idiotic idea I'd ever heard.

I looked at Spider as if he'd just told me to grow wings and fly back home. "Right!" I said. "Man, I'm dumb, but I'm not stupid. Why don't you drag him to the edge of the boom, and then *maybe* I'll see if we can pry the lure loose with a stick."

"OK, but don't hurt that lure. It was my grandpa's, you know," said Spider.

Although Spider's obvious concern for my welfare was touching, I didn't say anything. There wasn't time for sentimentality—I needed to concentrate. As Spider brought the turtle close to the boom's edge, Charlie handed me a stick he'd gotten from the bank. Taking the stick, I reached out and tried to tap the lure loose from the turtle's mouth. The turtle's jaws instantly clamped down on the stick like a vise. That hadn't been in our original plan, but I quickly formulated a Plan B.

I lifted the turtle out of the water, and headed toward the bank. Once on shore, I set the angry turtle onto the ground, but though I tried several tactics, he refused to let go of the stick, and the lure still dangled from the corner of his mouth.

As I reached out with my tennis shoe to nudge the animal in the back, I instantly learned several things about snapping turtles. First of all, they're not as slow as you might think. Second, they're actually quite agile, and third, they're well named.

In a heartbeat, the turtle's head shot out, his neck reaching far behind him and his jaws slicing completely through the end of my sneaker. Then, spitting out rubber and nylon, he turned and faced us menacingly.

"OK, guys, I think we need a new plan," said Spider.

"And a new pair of shoes," I added, looking down at my big toe, which was now plainly visible through the hole in my sneaker.

The turtle just stood there, quietly eyeing us—like a gunfighter waiting for his victim to make his move.

"You hold his head down with the stick, and then I'll reach out and grab the lure out of his mouth," Spider said.

Now that was a step in the right direction, it seemed to me. At least, there wouldn't be any parts of my own anatomy at risk with this plan. So I took the stick and pinned the turtle's head to the ground while Spider got down on his belly and crept slowly toward the struggling turtle.

It was at that moment that I learned several new lessons about snapping turtles. First, they're capable of using their front feet much like hands; and second, they're much stronger than you might think.

In a heartbeat, the turtle reached up with a front foot and pushed the stick away. Then he instantly turned his gaze to his left, where he found himself face-to-face with a very surprised Spider McGee. His eyes big as saucers, the big guy screamed, which seemed to startle the turtle, causing him to reach up with a front foot and pop the lure out of its mouth. Then it whirled around and scurried back toward for the river with amazing speed.

In the confusion, the lure leapt into the air, and when it came down, it lodged squarely in Spider's left ear. He began dancing around in pain, cussing and moaning, but we finally got him calmed down enough to cut the line and load him into the car.

It was a pitiful ride home. Charlie and I had to listen to Spider moaning in the backseat, and the only thing we could do was to look back at our whimpering friend, looking so pitiful, wearing what looked exactly like a giant hand-carved, bug-eyed Norwegian earring, then look back at each other—and laugh hysterically.

That whole incident took place some thirty years ago, and although Spider didn't know it at the time, he was a trendsetter. After all, he was the first guy I ever knew to wear an earring, even if he'd had to have his ear pierced by a snapping turtle in order to do it. I'm pretty sure they have easier ways of doing that nowadays.

June Weddings

As June wraps its arms around us like the warm hug of a favorite aunt, I find myself thinking about weddings…and one special afternoon on the bandstand. I've been a musician for thirty years, and I've played for scores of weddings and receptions, sometimes at more than one for the same person. For me, those gatherings were just another way to make my living—the money was good and there was usually decent food.

But as a wedding soloist, I never attended the rehearsals. I figured it would cut my hourly wages in half, and the person in charge of the rehearsal never let me do anything anyway. They'd stand on the stage in front of the altar, telling everyone what to do and when to do it, and when it came to the space where I would normally do my song, they'd just point to me and say, "And then you sing your song," and then keep right on going. So I stopped going to the rehearsals, since 90% of the time, I didn't know the people, and didn't need a meal badly enough to go out to supper afterward with a group of strangers I'd probably only meet that one time.

Sounds terribly mercenary, right? Well, it made perfect sense to me, and it only took attending a few such rehearsals to realize it was a waste of my time. I knew I could get the same information in less than five minutes the next day, as I walked into the church—an hour before the actual ceremony.

When the ceremony finally began, I'd sit off to the side, watching a bride in a white dress and a groom in the only rented tuxedo he would probably ever wear, promising to love each other forever. Part of me, deep inside, wanted to believe that every single one of those brides and grooms meant every word they were saying. After all, most of the time, people don't get married on a whim. Yet somehow, I couldn't shake a feeling of sadness that always seemed to wash over me as I watched that scene, knowing that one in every two of the marriages I witnessed were doomed to failure.

I can't explain the process, but over the years, I developed an eye for being able to know whether a bride and groom would make a go of their marriage or not. There was just something about the way the couple related to each other, the way they looked at each other and their body language that gave me clues as to how their union was going to turn out.

I got very jaded in my attitude, wondering why people continued to go through all the preparations, the pomp, circumstance, and expense, followed by the striving, the pain, and then the final agony of breaking up. I even went so far as to vow I would never get married myself, because it all seemed so hopeless.

Then one afternoon, all that changed.

Our band was playing for a large reception at a small town ballroom. I hadn't played at the wedding, so I hadn't seen the bride and groom. As I stood on the stage and sang, I casually looked across the vast sea of people. My glanced moved from table to table, until I found the bride and groom, sitting alone in a corner. They were sitting together with total ease, perfectly comfortable with each other, just watching the dancers, holding hands and saying nothing.

It struck me that the bride's flowing white dress and the groom's black tuxedo suddenly seemed out of place. Their happiness and comfort they felt with each other was totally apparent, unlike anything I'd ever seen. There was no question that those two people belonged together. It didn't matter what they were wearing. No matter what the situation, those two people would've been sitting in those same two chairs, still holding hands, even if they'd been dressed in blue jeans and overalls, attending the seventieth birthday party of somebody's else's favorite uncle.

Oh, they were at a party, to be sure…a big, loud party (our band was partly responsible for that) but it didn't matter. The party was really for the benefit of everyone else in attendance. It was a celebration—one they were happy to attend. But they didn't really need a party for themselves. They were totally comfortable just sitting in the corner, well out of the limelight, watching dozens of people they loved having a good time.

As cynical as I'd become over the years, something struck me at that moment, just watching that loving couple. I realized what the true meaning of a wedding ceremony is. Every wedding, in the truest sense of the word, represents the triumph of the human spirit. After all, every marriage is really a public statement made by two trusting individuals, standing before the world and announcing that they choose to believe in each other and the union they are about to create. Not only that, they are proclaiming that they believe their union will be the one-in-two that *lasts*. Seen in that light, every wedding really symbolizes the victory of hope…in the face of all odds.

Of course, it'll take all the courage and strength that bride and groom possess to beat the odds, but every year, millions of couples continue to try. It doesn't matter that most of them realize the odds are stacked against them. They continue to stand in front of friends and family and declare, "So what?" They choose to believe in the love and commitment they've expressed for each other, and you know what? Throughout history, human beings have staked their fortunes, and sometimes their very lives, on less than a 50-50 chance.

In the end, maybe that's why so many weddings are held in June. It's a month that's notoriously unpredictable—full of warmth and promise one moment, then suddenly becoming stormy and full of uncertainty the next. It's the perfect metaphor for the roller coaster ride every couple that chooses to get married will eventually have to face.

All I know for sure is the impact of seeing that loving couple holding hands at their reception had on me that June afternoon. Since that day, I've begun singing my wedding solos with a renewed sense of hope…hope embodied by the two people I see standing at the altar, their faces full of trust and love, vowing in front of their family and friends to move into the future together, as a married couple…in spite of the overwhelming odds.

Spelunking With Scooter

My youngest brother, Scooter, has always been the go-getter in our family. He got his first paper route at the age of four. It didn't matter that he couldn't read or ride a two-wheeler. He just tied the bundle of papers to the back of his tricycle with a rope and dragged them from house to house. Even though the newspapers were shredded to tissue paper by the time he got to the end of his route, Scooter had made his first fortune before he entered kindergarten.

Later in life, Scooter's main source of entertainment seemed to be dreaming up wild schemes, then roping me in and dragging me along, not unlike those bundles of newspapers, and sometimes I'd arrive at the end of the journey feeling almost as shredded. But I didn't really mind…one thing was sure: Scooter's adventures made life interesting.

One day, he came to me and announced, "Hey, Big Brother. I think we should learn to spelunk."

"Gesundheit," I said, thinking he was catching cold.

"No, *spelunk*," he explained. "Spelunking is a term for the process of exploring caves. And I know where there's a bunch of cool caves up by Silver Springs that we could look into. Who knows? We might even find a treasure or ancient artifacts while we were down there!"

I'd always thought ancient artifacts were notes you found in reference books about old paintings, but I didn't tell Scooter that. I did know what *treasure* was, though, so I agreed that, weird as the word might be, I was willing to try my hand at spelunking.

I discovered one nice thing right away. The sport of spelunking didn't have to cost very much money, which was an instant improvement from many of the schemes Scooter seemed to come up with, and that was good. The only thing we'd really need was a good flashlight, he said.

So we headed for the local hardware store. However, the guy at the store seemed to know something about the finer points of spelunking and assured us it was important to get the waterproof variety, even though they were three times more expensive than a regular flashlight. Although we didn't understand why at the time, we were soon to find out.

Flashlights in hand, we left the store and drove to Silver Springs, where I discovered that Scooter had been right—the area was riddled with caves. The trick now was to find one that looked just right. (The term "just right" meaning any cave with a mouth big enough for us to squeeze into without getting stuck.)

When we'd located the perfect cave, we stood for a moment in awkward silence, looking first at each other, and then down into the dark opening. Then Scooter said, "You should probably go in first. You're taller than me, so if you can stand up once you get inside, we'll know that I'll be able to stand up, too."

Hmmm...I thought about it for a few moments. This was Scooter's baby, and I was only supposed to be along for the ride. Still, I couldn't deny that his reasoning sounded logical, so with a nylon rope tied around my waist, I eased myself down into the cave, my feet groping for toeholds in the darkness. I finally found a ledge, and as I reached into my jacket for my flashlight, I suddenly learned why the activity is called spelunking.

As I fumbled around in my pocket, I first heard a tiny tinkling sound, then a silence, followed by the distinct sound of "spelunk" as

I heard my car keys falling into a pool of water somewhere in the inky darkness at the bottom of the cave.

The spelunking sound was immediately followed by a number of other, much louder sounds—coming from me as I let Scooter know I wasn't a very happy spelunker at that particular moment.

Hearing me rant, Scooter called down, "Hey, Big Brother, are you OK down there?"

"Yeah, I'm fine," I said through gritted teeth. "We'll talk about it later. Let's just say I'm just glad you drove."

"But I didn't drive—you did, remember?" Scooter said.

That bit of information caused me to add several more choice new words to my spelunking vocabulary, but I finally decided I had to refocus. After all, I was down in the hole now, and there was nothing I could do about it. Anyway, we just might get lucky and find some old art reference books, or whatever else it was we'd come looking for...my mind was a little cloudy at that point, trying not to think about having to hitchhike the forty miles back home to get my spare set of keys.

My immediate problem, though, was the fact that I couldn't see a thing. I reached into my jacket, fumbled around again and this time, I succeeded in pulling out my flashlight. But I hadn't planned on how wet it was going to be inside the cave, and just as I was flicking on my flashlight, it slipped from my fingers and tumbled, end over end, into the darkness below.

As I listened, I discovered that my flashlight made a similar noise to the one my car keys had made when they splashed into the water, but in a lower key and a bit less distinct. To be fair, though, I couldn't hear the flashlight's sound quite as well as I'd heard the first one, due to the "Oh, @#$%!" sound I was making myself at that moment.

Now what? I was now standing on a ledge, in total darkness, in a cave that I knew had a bottom, although how far down that bottom really was, I couldn't even guess, a rope around my waist, and a little brother who kept calling down, "Are you ready for me to come down yet, Big Brother?"

I seriously thought about telling Scooter to come down, just so I would have the pleasure of strangling him at that moment, but the incredible darkness suddenly seemed to close in on me, and then other things began to take on a higher priority...like survival.

Looking down, I could see my flashlight, shining dimly at the bottom of the pool, hundreds, maybe thousands, of feet below. I could barely estimate just how far down that bottom *really* was, and I can tell you—at that moment, my career as a spelunker officially ended! Any old art books that might have found their way down into that blackness would just have to wait to be discovered by someone else. And if there was any treasure down there, it was definitely safe for the time being—because I didn't care anymore. I made a vow that if the batteries in my flashlight held out, some other brave (or idiotic) person could use whatever light it might give off to find the treasure—and I'd gladly donate my share to their cause.

The only thing I wanted now was *out* of that darkness—and fast.

"Hold the rope, Scooter, I'm coming out!" I yelled as I began to climb back up toward the mouth of the cave.

"But I haven't even been inside yet," Scooter complained.

I didn't hear him—I was too busy scrambling like a scared spider up the side of the cave, headed toward the light. It seemed like hours before I emerged into the bright sunshine once more.

I pulled myself out of the hole and kissed the ground. But just as I stood up, I caught one last glimpse of the dense blackness inside that hole, and I could never be sure, but I saw the faint glint of something shiny through a watery glow at the bottom of the cave...it looked sort of like the beam of a waterproof flashlight, being reflected off a set of car keys.

Quality Time?

There's a phrase that has become popular over the past few years, one that fills me with wonder. That phrase is "quality time." We've all heard it, and for some reason, we all seem to accept it as a real concept. But to the average country person, it's a phrase that's difficult to comprehend.

Here's what I mean. Last summer, my 10-year-old son Cody and I spent an entire day walking the fields, checking fences. Whenever we saw a post that needed straightening or a strand of wire that needed to be tightened, we set right to work and fixed it.

Sweat poured down our faces, our shirts grew soaked from the hard work we were engaged in. But even as we strained against the task at hand, we talked about his little league baseball team and how he could improve his hitting to the opposite field.

Then, as we walked a little farther down the fence line, we laughed till we cried when a covey of quail nearly gave us a heart attack as they exploded out of the grass in front of us. We marveled at the amazingly varied call of a cardinal in the woods off to our right. We saw two red-tailed hawks circling lazily over our heads, and wondered about how it was possible for them to see field mice at such a height.

Yes, technically, we were working. But it was also a typical day for us: father and son. We weren't doing anything "special." And yet, I know from similar experiences I had with my own dad when I was

Cody's age that days just like that one will be the ones that came to mind when my son has grown up and has children of his own.

So I put it to you: was that "quality time?"

Before you answer, think back to your own childhood. What kinds of things do you remember most fondly about *your* parents? Was it the fact that your dad worked sixteen hours a day at the office, then fell asleep on the couch on the weekends because he was too exhausted from the week's work to do anything else?

No. I'm willing to wager those aren't the things you remember with the greatest fondness. More likely, your first memory is of the time you went for a walk along a country road in a warm summer rain, getting drenched to the bone, and then came home looking like not only something the cat had dragged in, but something the cat had dragged in, played with, and then forgotten under the refrigerator for a month.

You'll remember playing a simple game of catch in the back yard. You'll remember lying on your back on a silky summer night, hearing your dad tell you about the stars. You'll remember the time you caught your first bluegill, and your dad had to help take it off your hook…

Well, *your* kids feel the same way. Just like you did when you were a kid, even though you didn't know it at the time, your own children have a unique way of spelling the word "love."

They spell it…"t-i-m-e."

So the next time you find yourself promising you'll make it up to your daughter when she asks you to play "Chutes and Ladders" for the seven millionth time when you'd much rather watch the ball game, remember: your kids are watching *you*, too.

And no matter how young your kids are; they also know how to spell another important word: "quality." And strangely enough, your kids spell the word "quality" exactly the same way they spell "love."

Just like "love," they spell the word "quality"…"T-I-M-E."

The Bonfire

When I was a kid, there was one springtime ritual I always looked forward to. Once the warm weather finally looked like it had unpacked its suitcase and decided to stay awhile, it was time for the entire neighborhood to gather for the annual bonfire. By late afternoon, the crackling flames licked the sky, fanned by a warm breeze and fed by the amazing amount of debris that somehow seemed to reproduce beneath the snow every winter.

From time to time, a fireball would explode from the pile and go soaring into the air. It was quickly chased down by a group of the older kids and smothered with shovels amid gales of happy laughter. It was a giddy time, a celebration of sorts, really, our version of an ancient rite of spring, the burning of the old to make room for the new…new growth, new life, and new possibilities.

The bonfire burned far into the night, offering an occasion for us to gather around its orange glow and commune with each other amid the hypnotic dancing shadows. Though I didn't know it at the time, the glow of one particular bonfire would last in memory long after its embers had cooled to dust.

That year, we kids were playing hide and seek, just as we'd done many years before. My brother Jim and I lay on our stomachs in the grass some twenty yards from the blazing inferno, just at the edge of the immense darkness where we knew our younger cousins, brother and sister would not be brave enough to go.

Suddenly, I heard a sniff from somewhere in the shadows off to my right. I turned and saw several pairs of eyes reflecting the glow of the bonfire. It was about a dozen of our young cows, come to see what all the fuss was about. My brother and I looked at each other and though not a word was spoken, I knew we were both thinking the same thing.

We got up and moved slowly toward the cows, who shuffled back slightly, suspecting something. Then, with a quick movement, my brother lunged forward and leapt onto the back of the cow closest to him, his arms curling around the startled animal's neck in a viselike grip.

The cow's eyes took on a terrified look. Then it jerked forward and began to run…followed by a dozen other confused animals—straight toward the bonfire. I ran after the procession, hoping I could steer the herd away from the blaze, but running after them only made the cows more frightened.

A short time later, my brother realized that it might be prudent for him to part company with his wild-eyed steed. He leapt to the ground, and though he tried to help me turn them, the herd continued on their collision course with the happy crowd gathered around the fire.

I must admit, my recollection of the incident gets a little blurry from that point on. It was like being in the middle of some surreal nightmare where you're caught up in a storm of activity, but you can't move your legs. As Jim and I stood watching helplessly, we could see cattle leaping and darting, their eyes wild with fear, knocking over chairs and tables. Women were waving handkerchiefs, kids were yelling, men were cussing, and everyone was working to drive the frightened herd away from the fire. The whole scene was a mass tangle of confusion. One cow ran almost directly through the fire, emerging on the other side unscathed, like a firewalker in some sacred Hindu ceremony.

As we watched the unbelievable spectacle unfold, Jim and I stood paralyzed, barely able to comprehend what was happening. But then, it became obvious what we had to do next. We slowly edged our way back into the darkness, and then we made a wide circle, staying just at the edge of the light, until we emerged on the opposite side of the fire. We tore headlong into the fray, screaming and waving our hands as if we were just as surprised as anyone at this unexplainable outburst by our crazy cows.

Finally, as quickly as it had begun, the stampede was over. The cattle disappeared back into the night, and an eerie calm fell over the gathering, a little like that deafening silence that follows a tornado. The only sounds were the crackling fire, the occasional sob of a child, the sigh of a woman as she picked up the pieces of a shattered potato salad bowl off the ground, or a curse from one of the men.

"I can't understand what got into those cows," my grandpa said.

"Somethin' musta spooked 'em," said my uncle Bill.

Jim and I gave each other a cautious glance, but said nothing. There wasn't much we could have said, really. But we both knew one thing for certain: we were very glad that cows couldn't talk.

A Stitch In Time

Before I escaped the "Big City" and moved to rural Iowa, I spent a number of years as an appliance technician for a major retail company, repairing washers and dryers. It was a pretty good job, paid well and I got to drive around in a company truck all day, so each day was different.

During my time as a repairman, I discovered there were two kinds of customers. I called them "stayers" and "leaver-aloners." The stayers liked to hang around while you worked; talking to your feet while you lay on back, operating on their washer's underbelly. Stayers were OK, I suppose, but I must say that I preferred the leaver-aloners. They were the ones who generally met you at the door, led you to the laundry room, pointed to their broken machine and announced, "I'll be in the other room if you need me."

One cold winter afternoon, my last call of the day happened to be at a large house in an upper-middle class neighborhood. The house sat at the top of a fairly steep hill, on the end of an icy street. With such treacherous roads, I knew my truck wouldn't be able to make it to the top of their hill, so I parked at the bottom, grabbed my toolbox and walked up to the house. A nice-looking lady in her mid-30s met me at the door, and led me to the laundry room.

"Here's the washer," she said amiably. "I can't get it to spin."

Without another word, she took up a position by the doorway, leaned against the wall and began chatting amiably while I opened my toolbox and began making some preliminary tests on her machine. I was in the home of a stayer, it appeared. But I really didn't mind, since I discovered the problem quickly, knew it was nothing major and wouldn't take long to repair, even with the distraction of having someone talk to me while I worked.

Then something unexpected happened. As I bent over to move the washer away from the wall, the entire back of my pants split wide open. It was a very embarrassing situation for me, but to her credit, the woman simply said, "Oops! Looks like you've got a small problem there."

Although oops wasn't the word I would have chosen, I said, "Yes, ma'am, it appears that way. I'm sorry about that," trying to maintain my dignity in the face of an obviously ridiculous situation.

Without hesitation, she said, "Well, take them off."

"Excuse me?" I asked.

I guess I hadn't hidden my surprise very well, because she instantly added, "I mean, if you take them off, I can sew them up for you in no time at all."

I told her that even though I'd never seen it in the company manual, I was pretty sure my supervisor would frown on having one of his technicians performing appliance repairs in his underwear—but the lady was insistent.

"I understand that, and you're probably right. But what if I showed you to the bathroom. You could take off your pants in there, hand them to me through the door, and then I could sew them up for you. That should be all right, don't you think?"

I hesitated, but I had to get the repair done, and it really was a bit awkward the way things stood at the moment, so I followed the lady to the bathroom, where I dutifully removed my pants and handed them to her through a crack in the door. Then she disappeared—to her sewing room, I assumed—and I sat down on the toilet to wait.

Only a few minutes later, as I was thumbing through a magazine, I heard the front door open and a male voice call out, "Hi, Honey. I'm home!"

Oh no, it was her husband! Or maybe it wasn't her husband, in which case, it was someone else—somebody I didn't want to know about. Either way, I knew one thing for sure: this couldn't be good!

The woman made no answer as I heard the man shut the door. What was I going to do? I was trapped in the bathroom! My mind was racing, but I could come up with only two choices: I could either call out to him and tell him I was in his bathroom in my shorts, or I could sit still and hope he found his wife before he found me.

Even in my panicky state of mind, I immediately saw drawbacks to both plans. What if the guy was a cop or some other kind of guy who carried a gun? If I let him discover me in his bathroom, it was entirely possible he might shoot first and ask questions later. But if I called out to him and he was the hunter type, I could see that might be a problem, too. After all, even if he hadn't been armed when he'd walked in the door, there was no reason to believe he couldn't *get* armed fairly quickly before he came after me while I sat there in his bathroom, shaking like a raccoon in the headlights.

Although I didn't care much for my chances either way, I decided to wait. Surely, if there was a God in Heaven, the man would find his wife before he came into the bathroom and found me. I began to pray—since it looked like I was about to die anyway, it seemed like a good idea. After all, I figured, why wait till the last minute?

Suddenly, my panic was interrupted by a noise from just outside the bathroom window. A terrible thought struck me. Even though I'd heard the door shut, that didn't mean the man had come into the house. Maybe he'd gone back outside.

I decided I should probably peek out the window and see. But the window was too high for me to see out, so I stepped onto the side of the bathtub, stood on my tiptoes and began to inch my eyes above the sill.

Then I suddenly realized the folly of that idea. What if the man, or any of the neighbors, for that matter, saw me peeking through the bathroom window? What would they think? What *could* they think?

It all began to feel like a bad dream. I could almost feel my job beginning to become a distant memory. For that matter, it seemed like I *myself* was about to become only a distant memory, if I couldn't figure a way out of this mess!

So I decided it was a better idea *not* to look out the window, after all. I lowered myself back down till I was firmly perched on the side of the tub. But when I turned around…I saw the figure of a huge hulk of a man, standing in the doorway—and he did *not* look happy.

I've heard of people talking in tongues while in the midst of spiritual rapture, but at that moment, I also found myself stammering in some strange foreign language. "Look, mister, this isn't as bad as it looks," I finally managed to say.

"*Nothing* could be as bad as this looks," he said in a menacing tone.

I carefully climbed down from the edge of the tub and stood looking up at this towering figure, waiting for my life to end. But he didn't move or say a word. He just stood there, arms folded across his massive chest. I must say, I found a little relief in the fact that he appeared to be unarmed. But just as I was about to make a run for it, pants or no pants, the woman appeared in the doorway, holding my pants in her hand.

"OK, Jack, this has gone far enough," she said. "Let's just give the poor man his pants so he can get back to work."

To my surprise, Jack began to laugh. "Boy, fella. I'll bet you thought you were a goner for sure, huh, guy?"

I was confused. Was I reading the situation correctly? Was I really going to live through this?

Jack laughed again. "My wife told me the whole story when I came in, but I just couldn't resist playing a little joke on you," he explained. "I hope you don't mind."

He took my pants from his wife's hands and held them out. "Here you go. Linda's a great seamstress. You'll never know they were ripped. Are you sure you're OK? You don't look too good."

I was still shaking as I took the pants from his massive hands. I said, "I think so, but the way you scared me, I can tell you one thing: it's lucky for me I was in the bathroom!"

Once I had regained what was left of my composure and gotten dressed, we all had a good laugh about the whole thing while I finished the repair job. But as I drove back to the shop, I knew it wasn't a call I'd forget any time soon.

Before I finally left the repair business to become a fulltime writer, I would have a number of other unusual experiences. But I can tell you one thing for certain: not one of those other episodes would ever involve being trapped in a strange woman's bathroom in my underwear!

Notes On Perfection

As winter closes in around us, I sometimes find myself looking wistfully out of the window at the spot where my flower garden sits beneath the snow, waiting for spring to return.

In my younger days, I used to think planting flowers was a complete waste of time. I didn't mind tending a big vegetable garden and spending lots of time nurturing my beans, cucumbers and tomatoes. After all, I figured, one day all my hard work would pay off, yielding fruit that would help sustain my body. But what would flowers ever do for me? You couldn't eat them, so they couldn't help keep me alive, although I had read somewhere that there were a couple edible flowers, but I couldn't remember which ones they were. It just seemed like planting flowers represented a whole lot of work for nothing, if you would have asked me then.

It was not until years later that I finally realized how flowers also could sustain me, but in a very different sense. Over time, I began to understand that flowers nurtured a special place inside, a place that only beauty could satisfy. Although it had nothing to do with sustaining my physical body, flowers satisfied something more etheric, something difficult to explain, inside my soul. Since I made that discovery, flowers have always been a part of my garden scheme.

Yesterday, while looking out at the snow-covered marigolds and geraniums, I found myself thinking back to an incident from last summer. I had been sitting on the porch, admiring the beauty of my multi-colored flowers in the garden and reflecting about how perfect the day was, when something suddenly occurred to me. Of all the things in this world, I thought, surely flowers must represent the best example of perfection.

I got up, walked to the garden, knelt down and began to examine the flowers closely, but what I found was a surprise. No matter how hard I tried, I couldn't find a single blossom that I judged to be an example of a "perfect" flower. Most of them were asymmetrical, their petals were twisted, and the colors that had seemed so brilliant from my vantage point on the porch now seemed dull and mundane. Although I looked for a long time, I couldn't find a perfect flower among the entire lot.

As I sat there among my beloved flowers, I felt a sense of melancholy sweep over me. I felt let down somehow. I had counted on these blossoms to teach me a spiritual lesson, and they had left me disappointed. I felt betrayed. How could these flowers look so perfect from a distance, and then turn out to be such a disappointment when I examined them closely?

I sat there thinking for a long time, until I suddenly began to understand. My flowers were indeed perfect, just as they were. It was my perception that was faulty. I was seeking a form of perfection that didn't exist in the real world. These flowers were perfect examples of what they were, which was simply flowers…nothing more, nothing less, and that's all they really needed to be, no matter what I thought. As flowers, they were perfect!

Suddenly, I began to see my entire flower garden with new eyes. It didn't matter that it was a crazy quilt of reds, blues and purples, violating every accepted rule of color coordination, and that some of the plants sported flower heads far too big for their spindly stems. It also didn't matter that some of the flowers were delightful to look at, but smelled like old shoes. None of that made any difference!

My flowers showed me a thousand ways to be imperfect that summer afternoon. There wasn't a single one of them that lived up to my preconceived notion of the ideal flower. Yet as I sat there, the simple act of looking at them made me glad, even in the midst of their imperfection, and it made me smile. My flowers were simply being the best examples of what they had been created to be, in the best way they knew how…and that was enough.

Need Some Help Cowboy?

Although I've never been one to put much stock in clichés, I learned the truth of one particular adage, "A friend in need is a friend, indeed," first-hand one day...at a rodeo.

It was the early 1980s, and everyone in America seemed to be caught up in a cowboy craze that had swept the nation after the release of the film "Urban Cowboy." My brothers Jim, Dan and I, being entrepreneurs, decided to cash in on the fad by buying a mechanical bull exactly like the one that had been featured in the movie.

To our great joy, our bull was an immediate smash hit, and since we'd modified our bull to be able to move it from location to location, we were quickly booked solid for a full year, playing to huge crowds of would-be bull riders at charity functions, county fairs, night clubs, and rodeos. We went anywhere someone would pay us to go, even carrying the monster up two flights of stairs one day for an engagement at a health club.

Everyone, it seemed, was eager to try their hand at tackling our mechanical beast. Everywhere we went, we were surrounded by wannabe cowboys and cowgirls decked out in cowboy hats, blue jeans and colorful western shirts. It didn't matter that the nearest "wide open space" was the paved parking lot at the local mall. The entire country was infected with a wild case of "mechanical bull fever," and my brothers and I were poised and ready to cash in.

And cash in, we did. The money flowed in like water over a dam, faster than we could count it. The pockets of our jeans, shirts and western-style jackets bulged with dollar bills being handed to us by eager riders. For us, the machine wasn't just a mechanical bull—it was a cash cow.

But after awhile, we began to get bored with the actual riding of the machine, since we could ride as much as we wanted. We put together some tricks and began doing demonstrations for the crowds that always surrounded us. We learned to ride with no hands. But we found ourselves beginning to wonder if we might not be ready to try our hand at the riding real thing. That curiosity was made even more intense by the almost universal scorn we received from the "real" cowboys and cowgirls at the various rodeos where we set up. Those folks saw us a freak show, and though we wouldn't have admitted it to anyone, secretly we believed they were right. It didn't matter how much money we were making—we were a joke to the real rodeo people, and that hurt.

One night, Jim and I decided it was time to find out, once and for all, if we could ride genuine rough stock. So the next morning, I was appointed to go to the rodeo office and see how we could go about entering a rodeo event we thought would be perfect for us. It was called the Wild Horse Scramble, which involved releasing eight wild horses into the arena at once, each carrying a novice or wannabe cowboy on its back. The event was a real crowd pleaser, wild and crazy, with horses and dislodged cowboys flying everywhere…sort of a flesh, fur and blood fireworks display, designed to start the rodeo off with a bang.

But for Jim and I, entering the Wild Horse Scramble meant something more. It meant being able to try our hand at riding real rough stock, without risking total humiliation, since no one expected any of the riders in the Wild Horse Scramble to stay aboard, anyway. If we fell off, that was expected; there'd be no shame—it seemed like a win-win situation.

So early the next morning, totally decked out in my best cowboy outfit, I set out for the fairgrounds gate. But I discovered I would have to pay to get into the fairgrounds, even though all I wanted was information about how to enter the Wild Horse Scramble. It seemed unfair to me to have to pay for something like that, and since I've always had a well-developed flair for righteous indignation, I decided to sneak in. (I didn't matter how much money we'd raked in the night before…there was a principle of fairness involved here, and I've always been a person who bristled at injustice.)

My plan was simple: I'd walk along the edge of the eight-foot-high mesh wire fence that surrounded the fairgrounds until I found a place where I could climb over. Since it was early in the morning, no one would witness my act of defiance. No one would be harmed, I figured, since all I was going to do was ask for information and then walk straight back to our camp, so it seemed like a reasonable plan.

I walked along the fence, looking for a likely spot to climb over. When I found it, I quickly scaled the wire. But just as I was swinging my back leg over the top of the fence, I lost my balance and fell forward. I put my arms out to break my fall, but the heel of my boot caught in the fence and I came to an abrupt halt, about five feet from the ground.

I suddenly found myself hanging upside down from the fence, dangling like a prize marlin on a boat dock. My boot was wedged solid. I couldn't move, and I couldn't reach the ground. There was nothing I could do but hang there like a fool until someone came to my rescue. But I knew that no matter who that someone might happen to be, there was no doubt it was going to be embarrassing—for me and my brothers.

After all, if it was a security guard who found me, I'd have to confess that I'd been trying to sneak into the fairground just to save a lousy $3.00, even though I had a hundred times more than that in my wallet. If it was a rodeo person who found me, I'd instantly become living proof that the guys who ran that mechanical bull really were the lame knuckleheads everyone already suspected.

As I hung from the fence like a limp dishrag, contemplating my misfortune, I suddenly heard a deep voice saying, "Hey, partner, looks like you could use a little help."

I strained my neck to see who was talking to me and saw a tall, good-looking cowboy on a buckskin mare.

I said, "Yeah, I think you're right. My boot seems to be stuck." (I tried to sound nonchalant, but it's hard to make casual conversation when you're hanging upside down from an eight-foot fence.)

Without dismounting, the cowboy inched his horse closer to the fence, then reached out and untangled my boot from the wire. I crashed to the ground like a sack of chicken feed being tossed off the back of a pickup truck.

I stood there for a while, tentatively shaking various parts of my anatomy to see they were all still attached. When I was satisfied that everything was still functional, I looked up at my rescuer and immediately went into shock. The man I was looking at wasn't a mere cowboy. This man was currently leading the world in the overall standings; and was one of the finest bull riders in the history of rodeo. It was a man I'd seen on TV dozens of times and had admired for years.

Instantly, I wished I was still hanging on the fence. After all, the fate of my poor brothers and I was now sealed. As soon as this world-champion cowboy, loved and respected by everyone, began to tell this story to anyone who would listen, we'd never be able to show our faces on a rodeo grounds again.

I don't know why, but I felt compelled to tell him exactly how I'd come to be hanging from that fence in the first place, about the unfairness of having to pay to get in, and anything else I could think of that might convince this stranger that I wasn't the complete loser I appeared to be at that moment.

To his credit, the cowboy listened patiently as I stammered, and then said, "Listen, partner, you didn't have to go through all that! All you had to do was to go around to the rodeo entrance at the back of the fairgrounds and tell 'em you wanted to enter the Wild Horse Scramble. They woulda letcha right in."

Hmmm...as unbelievable as it seemed, the thought that there might be a special entrance for rodeo participants had never crossed my mind. I'd been so caught up in the injustice of having to pay at the front gate that I guess my brain had stopped thinking altogether. As the blood slowly began to leave my head and move back into the rest of my body, I realized that I'd gotten so focused on that one solution that I hadn't weighed any other options.

Chuckling softly, the cowboy held out his hand and said, "Swing on up here, partner, and I'll give you a ride over to the rodeo office."

To a rodeo fan, this was like having St. Peter reach down and say, "Hey, would you like a little tour of Heaven?" And since I wasn't sure I could walk, anyway, I grabbed his hand and swung up behind the lean cowboy.

As we rode across the pasture parking lot, he said, without looking back, "Man, you're lucky I found ya. You're one of those guys who run the mechanical bull, aren't you? You know, a thing like that might get around and it could turn out to be kinda embarrassing for you."

Although he hadn't said it out loud, I heard what he was saying, and it filled me with admiration for this compassionate cowboy. I knew in that moment that I was dealing with not only a world-champion cowboy, but a world-class human being, as well.

When we reached the rodeo office, he gently lowered me to the ground. Then, as he turned his horse and began riding back toward the rodeo arena, he turned and called out, "Good luck, cowboy!"

I was stunned, standing there with those words echoing through my mind. He'd called me "cowboy!" The All-around Champion of the World had called me a cowboy! It was one of the most incredible moments of my life. I watched him ride away, then turned and walked into the rodeo office with a new sense of confidence. After all, I was a *cowboy*, and doggone it, I belonged there…and that very night, my brother Jim and I rode in the Wild Horse Scramble.

That all took place more than twenty years ago, but it left a lasting impact. Neither Jim nor I continued to ride in the rodeo. We quickly learned that there was much more money to be made with our mechanical bull, without getting ourselves banged up like those cowboys who dare to challenge real flesh-and-blood rough stock every night. After all, our bull had an on/off switch for when we got in trouble!

Sadly, the "urban cowboy" craze died out soon after that. We sold our bull and moved on to other pursuits. But every time I look at my son, Cody, now a fine young man in his own right, I think about that world-champion cowboy he's named after, and a simple act of kindness a cowboy offered me so long ago. And whether it's a tired old cliché or not, I know for sure that sometimes "a friend in need" truly can turn out to be a friend indeed…even to a guy who happens to be hanging upside from a fence the first time they meet.

Dad's Fishin' Pole

One of the first lessons we learn in life is that our life experience actually consists of both hills and valleys, and that sometimes you get close-up views of both...in an unbelievably short period of time. I learned that lesson early in life—while on a fishing trip with my dad.

We were on vacation at Dad's favorite lake, and I was manning the oars while he fished the edge of a field of lily pads for bass. For as long as I could remember, that had been my role—Dad fished, I rowed. But that was enough for me. Just being part of the experience was magical, watching Dad's mastery of rod and reel, his accuracy in putting the lure anywhere he chose, working it just right, then setting the hook and bringing a big bass up to the boat.

But that year, something unbelievable happened. When we'd finally pulled up to his favorite fishing spot, Dad looked at me and said, "You wanna try it, Son?"

I was stunned. If he had said, "You wanna get out of the boat, walk across the water and get our lunch?" I couldn't have been more surprised.

"Sure, Dad," I stammered. As I reached out my hands, my dad handed his brand-new rod and reel to me, like Merlin handing Excalibur to Arthur. It was almost like an out-of-body experience. I held the translucent green pole out in front of me, my mind reeling from the significance of this incredible moment.

We were sitting about thirty yards from shore, in a spot where the water was deep and green. I took the rod in my right hand and prepared for my first-ever cast into the field of lily pads, taking one last glance over at my father, just to make sure I wasn't sitting in the boat with a space alien who'd somehow taken over my dad's body. But he just sat there, watching me, smiling as his eldest son prepared to join the ranks of real bass fishermen.

I smiled back, held out my right hand and deftly flipped the rod forward, like I'd seen my dad do a thousand times. In a heartbeat, the pole slipped from my hand, soared into the air and plopped into the lake. Then, in the blink of an eye, it was gone beneath the water.

For a moment, the world stood still. For a moment, I wished my Dad had been a space alien. At least then he could have zapped me into oblivion and put me out of my misery. I thought briefly about jumping in after the pole. It didn't matter that I couldn't swim…even drowning was preferable to having to turn and face my Dad at that moment.

But when I finally got the courage to look at him, I was surprised to see that Dad was amazingly calm. He didn't say a word; in fact, he seemed to have been struck mute. I could see his lips moving, but no sound came out. That was fine, though, because in my state of mind at that moment, I don't think I could have understood any known human language, anyway.

We sat in utter silence—for what seemed like a very long time. Dad had bought that pole especially for this trip. He and I had spent the entire winter pouring over fishing catalogs to find the perfect combination of rod and reel. And this trip was to be the inaugural launch of this new outfit. But now, it was all gone, sitting at the bottom of the lake.

I looked away, staring across the lily pads, waiting for whatever was going to happen next. Then I heard Dad moving around in the front of the boat. I was afraid to look, but I could hear him picking up an oar. This was it, I thought, and it would be justifiable homicide. After all, once they heard the whole story, no jury in the world would convict him!

But to my surprise, Dad took the oar and plunged the broad end of the oar into the water. In a moment, I saw what he was doing. There, a few feet from the boat, floating alongside a large lily pad, was a fishing lure!

Though I hadn't noticed in my excitement, Dad had tied a floating lure to the line before handing me the pole. In a few seconds, he had snagged the lure with the oar, and lifted it out of the water. Then, as Dad pulled the line into the boat hand-over-hand, the pole finally emerged from the depths of the lake.

Looking back on that experience, with the benefit of forty years, both as a fisherman and a man, I suspect my dad had probably tied that floating lure to the line on purpose, just in case of such a disaster. But I never asked him, and he's never told me.

I've been fishing thousands of times since that day, and I've lost enough tackle to stock a mid-sized bait shop, but I can honestly say none of those fishing trips ever caused me more panic than I felt that day on the lake with my dad, so long ago. But you know, I also remember the other lesson I learned that day. Sometimes, it's a short trip from the mountaintop to the valley of despair and back again—sometimes it can happen in the blink of an eye, or the flash of a bass lure, floating beside a lily pad in a quiet lake on a summer morning.

Take A Hike!

At one time, I was a jock and worked out every day. I want to make that clear right up front. But that seems like several centuries ago. In the past few years, the only exercise I got was mental exercise…that is, thinking about getting back in shape.

Then, I discovered another form of exercise…an exercise in torture. It happened every time I looked in the mirror. I had to force myself to look at my reflection and believe me, it wasn't pretty. Wherever a human body could droop, I drooped…especially around the midsection. I had developed the early symptoms of the dreaded "Dunlap disease" (you know, that disease in which your belly "dunlap" over your belt).

As far as endurance goes, forget it. I couldn't climb a flight of stairs without having a paramedic close by my side. For me, "second wind" was something brought on by a bowl of hot chili.

Finally, I'd had enough, and I resolved to do something about it. I began to accumulate every piece of exercise equipment I saw on those infomercials the TV stations show on Saturday afternoons between real sports seasons. I bought climbers, rollers, gliders, bikers, skiers, skaters, strollers, benders, shapers…you name it. If it was on TV, it was in my rec room—and I hated them all. They were used mainly as things to hang my clothes on when I was in a hurry. And if the clothes hadn't been on them, that equipment would have been covered with dust.

But then I discovered an activity that's not only fun, burns calories and gets me outside, but costs next-to-nothing! I took up hiking. That's right: plain old, nothing special, nothing fancy, anybody-can-do-it hiking.

I know, hiking sort of went out of fashion a few years back, and I suspect it's been neglected by the mainstream media for a number of reasons.

1) Hiking doesn't require $6,000 worth of special equipment just to get started…like $900 shoes, for instance. That being the case, equipment makers can't plaster their company logos on armloads of specialized gear that a hiker "simply has to have" before they leave the house. When you go out hiking, you can wear pretty much whatever you want, according to your own style and pocketbook. Why, it's practically un-American in that respect!

2) Hiking is usually done either solo or with a couple friends. There's no 24-second clock, no home runs, no touchdowns. In fact, it resists lending itself to being organized into teams altogether—and with no teams of any kind, there can be no professional teams. With no professional teams, there can be no professional leagues for those teams to play in, which means no superstars. And with no superstars, there are no endorsements for mega companies to use to sell all sorts of expensive equipment. (If you're confused by all this, please refer back to 1.)

There is another, more down-to-earth reason why folks have strayed away from hiking, which has to do with where the majority of Americans now live…in big cities. In cities, places to hike are often limited, and people are forced to hike through city parks. The problem with hiking through a big city park is that it can sometimes lead to other more strenuous activities, such as mugger wrestling or sprinting for your life in order to escape some other type of unsavory character.

So with all those factors going against it, it's not surprising that hiking has pretty much fallen by the wayside for many folks. But that doesn't mean hiking isn't still great exercise, assuming you can find a nice place to do it. But for the sake of our discussion, let's assume you have found such a spot. (I promise, they do exist. All you have to do is look for them.) And once you've found your hiking spot, here are a few suggestions for getting the most out of your hiking experience.

First, choose your hiking buddies carefully. Look for partners you'll be able to tolerate for long periods, because you're going to be hiking beside these people for hours at a stretch. Believe me, there's nothing that can spoil an otherwise pleasant day on the trail more that having your thoughts torn between the beauty of the scenery and the notion of strangling an obnoxious hiking companion with your bare hands.

Once you've chosen your partners, be sure to keep your hiking speed at a comfortable level. The general rule for pacing yourself is similar to jogging, which suggests maintaining a tempo that allows you to carry on a normal conversation while you're hiking. (A word of advice: "Huh, huh, huh, gasp, wheeze, cough" *does not* count as normal conversation.)

Another warning. Never hike an advanced trail with a kid who tells you he's the "monkey bar champ" of his third grade class…you're only asking for trouble.

As you're straining your way up a steep grade, I can assure you that kid will become an annoyance, bouncing around you and saying things like, "Isn't this great? Don'tcha just love the uphill parts? The steeper, the better, I think, don't you? What's the matter? You don't look too good."

In that case, you'll find yourself tempted to respond with a witty comment, such as, "Huh, huh, huh, gasp, wheeze, cough," but watch yourself, because we've already established a comment like that as being improper etiquette.

And finally, when you're hiking, forget about looking cool. There's usually no one around to see you, anyway, and it's hard to look cool when you're leaning into a hill the size of Mt. McKinley and breathing so hard that your lungs seem to be trying to climb outside your body and go it alone. That's another reason why choosing your hiking companions is so important—because if you've chosen carefully, they'll never notice your plight. They'll be too busy with breathing problems of their own, and be so involved with simply trying to survive that they'll never notice whether you look cool or not.

So there you have it. If you're looking for an interesting, healthy way to exercise, think about hiking. Even though it's been long ignored, you may find hiking to be the perfect way to rebuild a tired, out-of-shape body. I'll be happy to recommend it, as long as you don't ask me while we're out on the trail, hiking up a steep grade. (That is, of course, unless you can understand the meaning of, "Huh, huh, huh, gasp, wheeze, cough.")

Opal's China

Since I was our family's first grandchild, my mom's sisters all became surrogate mothers for me. It was like having five mothers. So each year, as Mother's Day rolls around, I sometimes find myself feeling a bit lost, being 2000 miles away from my nearest "mom."

But since I moved to rural Iowa, there's a neighbor lady up the road who has helped me cope with those feelings by taking me under her wing. Her name is Opal Endersen, a wonderful, sweet older woman, much wiser than she believes herself to be.

A few days before Mother's Day last year, I was sitting at the kitchen table in Opal's farmhouse. We were just talking about nothing in particular when she brought me a plateful of her amazing brownies. They were all arranged in a circle on a lovely old plate that was beautifully illustrated with a winter farm scene.

I laughed. "Hey, Opal, I'm family, remember? You know you don't have to break out the good china to feed me."

She just smiled and said softly, "That's not special stuff. That's our everyday china. I got it for Mother's Day over twenty years ago."

"Wow, it looks pretty fancy for every day stuff," I said.

Carrying two steaming cups of coffee in her hands, Opal joined me at the table.

"You know," she said, "I've never believed in putting your best things away for special occasions. After all, if you think about it, what's more special than your family? Aren't they what make life special? And if they are, why shouldn't they be the ones who get to share the joy of using your good china?"

Opal's words struck home as I found my mind drifting back to an incident involving my great-aunt Maude, a lovely woman who'd passed away several years ago. Maude had never married, and lived alone all her life. But she was a very generous woman, spending her entire life working for various charitable organizations, helping thousands of needy people over the course of her long lifetime.

Yet, after Maude died, I was amazed by the conversation that took place while I helped my parents, aunts and uncles sort through the belongings in Maude's house.

"Look at this! It's that silver serving tray Rene and I gave her for her 75th birthday," my uncle Bill said, "and it's still in the box!"

"And here's that set of silverware Winn and I gave her for Christmas; it must have been ten years ago. It doesn't look like it's ever been used," said Aunt Nora.

Time after time, we ran across gifts Maude had been given by loving friends and relatives, but never used. The more unopened gift boxes we discovered, the sadder it all seemed, and the clearer it became how Maude had looked at the world throughout her long life.

Every time Maude had received a beautiful gift from someone, she had tucked it away for use at some "special occasion." But it seemed that for Maude, that special occasion never arrived, and the gift, which had been so lovingly given, had never been used.

As I sat in Opal's kitchen, thinking of my aunt Maude, I began to examine the plate Opal had set on the table more carefully. I immediately saw that it had a fairly large chip on the edge.

"Doesn't it hurt a little bit to see your best china getting all chipped up while you use it for every day?" I asked.

Silently, Opal stood and held out her hand. I stood, too, and she led me over to the sink. She reached up, opened a cabinet the door and pulled out a cracked coffee cup, which bore the same pattern as the plate of brownies.

"This coffee cup got cracked the day Matt went off to join the Navy," she said.

Then she pulled out another plate, saying, "And the chip on this plate happened the morning Sasha got married."

One by one, Opal pulled out various dishes, saucers and plates, telling me the story behind each chip and crack. Finally, she took out one last cup and silently held it for a long moment, tears forming in her eyes. She said nothing, and although I didn't ask, there was no doubt that cup held a very special memory, perhaps the most poignant memory of all.

Wiping her eyes, she finally turned to me and said, "You see, this isn't just our good china. It's not even our everyday china. It's really the history of our family. And if I hadn't used it every day, all that wonderful, precious history would've been lost."

It was a lovely moment, and as I walked toward home along the gravel road that afternoon, thoughts of my aunt Maude, and the story of Opal's china kept swirling around in my mind. And before I reached our farm, I'd come to a decision. Tonight, we'd eat supper off our own good china. It didn't make any difference what was on the menu…tonight would be a special occasion.

The Striped Cardinal

Whenever I visit our local grade school for an open house nowadays, I find myself scanning the hallway walls for crayon-colored pictures of striped cardinals. And every time I see one, I know exactly what was going through the mind of that boy or girl when they began coloring their picture.

You see, we also had to color similar pictures of cardinals when I was in grade school. And the teacher always told us to concentrate on two specific things: first, try to stay inside the lines, and second, make sure to color your cardinal red.

Now, I was all right with the "staying between the lines" part. That made sense, and it was even a skill that would serve me well later in life, especially when I learned to drive a car. But something inside me rebelled against the idea that a cardinal had to be red. After all, I'd never seen a cardinal before, so until I actually could prove it with my own eyes, I could see no reason why a cardinal couldn't be some other color. And who really knew for sure? Somewhere in some remote part of the world, still waiting to be discovered, there might have actually been a species of cardinals with stripes.

Therefore, I reasoned, in spite of all the energy my teacher expended trying to persuade me otherwise, that just because I had never personally seen a striped cardinal, that didn't mean they didn't exist. After all, I'd never seen red one either, and she seemed to be intent on trying to convince me *they* were real!

After living for many years, and gathering a great deal of experience, I've come to realize it's those things that are different in the world, the striped cardinals, if you will, that tend to catch our eye, and it's those very differences that make those striped cardinals special.

For example, remember that night you went to a local talent show and one of the acts featured twenty eight-year-olds, all kicking their chubby little legs for dear life in a chorus line? But there was always one little girl on the far left, completely out of step, yet blithely going about her business as if it was really those other nineteen kids who needed to get with the program. Whether you felt embarrassed for her or thought she was just too darling for words, I guarantee it was that one girl…the striped cardinal…you remembered as you walked out of the gym that night.

I encountered another example of a striped cardinal a few weeks ago—at a high school football game. Our school's marching band was on the field, doing their best to stay in step, hit their marks, watch out for each other, while trying to play their instruments at the same time. The entire band was dressed in their beautiful new white uniforms with high white caps, all topped with red feathers…except one young man. For whatever reason, his uniform was identical to everyone else's except for his cap, which was topped by a white feather. It made no sense. Why would one boy's hat be different from all the rest? He was simply playing a sousaphone, so he wasn't the leader.

But you know, try as I might, I couldn't stop watching that white feather as it bounced about on that boy's head. I tried chastising myself for being so petty. What was wrong with me? After all, I was the guy who knew all about striped cardinals. In this case, there were even feathers involved! So I, of all people, should realize how wrong it was to become obsessed with that one boy, simply because he was wearing a different-colored feather from everyone else.

Then it hit me: I was looking at the situation all wrong. That one boy with the white feather in his cap was living proof of our human tendency to take special notice of the unusual. After all, it's not the nameless person in the crowd, looking or acting exactly like everyone else who will one day be honored with a statue in the local city park. Chances are, the person receiving such an honor will have been the girl kicking out of step, the boy with the white feather in his cap…or the kid who colors stripes on his cardinal in preparation for an open house.

We all have times in our lives when we feel out of step, out of tune with our surroundings. And yet, it's often at those exact times when something deep inside insists that the way we're doing it really is the right way for *us*, regardless of how the rest of the world might see it.

What we're really doing during those special moments in our lives is creating our version of a striped cardinal.

So whenever you find yourself feeling out of step with your chorus line, take a moment to stop and listen…and then go with what your heart tells you. Because it's at those moments when you have a chance to be something very important…yourself.

There are millions of red cardinals in the world. Everyone knows that, right? Well maybe…but when a striped one finally *is* discovered, you'll be able proudly point to it and say, "I knew they'd find it! After all, I've already *seen* one."

Some Thoughts on Email

Since I've been online, I have begun to do almost my entire correspondence via email. I know I'm not alone in that, but I've begun to notice some subtle changes and some frustrations in dealing with email that I never expected.

For instance, the first thing I've noticed with email is that it's more difficult to know when it's my turn to write. It used to be that when I received a letter from someone, I put it on the corner of my desk and left it there until I got around to writing a return letter. But with email, there is no setting the envelope aside to remind you it's your turn every time you sit down to work. No, emails just lurk around somewhere on the hard drive, never giving any visual clues that you've shirked your duty.

Getting email letters or electronic cards from kids can be an exercise in frustration, too. After all, you can't stick those things in a manila envelope for reminiscing over 25 years from now, and I can assure you that sticking them onto the refrigerator is quite a chore, as well. Think of the kind of magnet you'd have to use to stick a 17" monitor onto the refer door!

I admit, there are some very nice things about email, too. You can get email on Sundays, and you can send messages back and forth with someone several times during the course of a single day, but I have to say, I've never had a #10 envelope crash right in the middle of a long, heartfelt letter, forcing me to start over from scratch.

Another noticeable difference is that every email looks pretty much identical. Email has pretty much done away with the sometimes not-so-subtle differences in people's handwriting. Of course, it works the other way, too. For instance, I've personally gotten at least 15 emails thanking me for not using a pen and paper anymore, since my writing style has been variously described as somewhere between hieroglyphics and the scrawl of a 3-year-old with the shivering shakes.

All in all, though, I think the advantages of email outweigh the disadvantages. In my own case, I can email my articles to various magazines quickly and cheaply (which is always a good thing for a freelance writer, since our income is usually somewhere between miniscule and nonexistent). On the downside, though, I can't scan rejection letters for subtle clues as to why an editor declined one of my pieces, which are often to be found in the tiny handwritten notes scrawled in the margins.

So here's to the email revolution. Like it or not, we'll all eventually have to learn to live with the new technology, and to readjust our thinking when it comes to refrigerator art or dusty "in boxes" on the corners of our desks.

Batter Up!

With the arrival of spring, America's scenery begins to change. It's not the greening of lawns, or the blooming of spring flowers. It's the sight of kids and their parents…playing catch. From coast to coast, it seems Americans have always been in love with the game of baseball.

And over the years, our movies have reflected our love for the game. In fact, 1998 was a landmark year for the relationship between baseball and film. That year marked the 100th anniversary of baseball on film, beginning with Thomas Edison's 1898 short, "The Ballgame," which featured a scrimmage between two local amateur teams.

American moviegoers can't seem to get enough films based on our national pastime, and that's understandable, because the game lends itself perfectly to the silver screen. Since Edison's first baseball film, more than 100 movies have also tried to capture the drama and humor of America's favorite summer ball game.

The game of baseball embodies America's eternal spirit of hope and optimism. "It ain't over till it's over," said former New York Yankee great, Yogi Berra, and the many films made over the years have reflected that belief over an entire century.

There's also high drama inherent in a grand slam or a shoestring catch. In "The Natural" (1984), Robert Redford literally comes back from the dead, belts a homer of mythic proportions and runs the bases amid a transcendent shower of sparks. Steve Martin's son makes a miracle catch in "Parenthood" (1989) while his father dances wildly, caught up in the sheer joy of the moment. The tears we shed during those scenes are a combination of hope and simple joy at the triumph of the individual in the face of all obstacles.

But baseball also has lots of room for comedy. (The wonderful 1949 "It Happens Every Spring" comes to mind.) Even William Shakespeare understood the comedic potential of the game, calling one of his most famous works "A Comedy of Errors," about a bumbling group of Elizabethan ballplayers on a long road trip.

The quintessential baseball movie, "Field of Dreams" (1989), was produced near the town of Dyersville, Iowa. It deals with fathers and sons, unresolved emotions and unrealized dreams, bringing all those complex themes into dramatic focus by staging the action around a baseball diamond. And the final scene was a powerful summary of how all Americans would love their own dreams to end...with the possibility of a brighter future.

Even after more than a decade, the Dyersville Chamber of Commerce still sends out nearly a quarter million tourist brochures every year, largely due to the lasting appeal of "Field of Dreams."

Years after the film's release, the field is still surrounded by an almost mystical atmosphere. Fathers walk to the pitcher's mound and stand quietly, absorbed in their private memories. Then they gently toss a ball to a young child standing at the plate. There's no formal structure to the "Field of Dreams" experience. It's strictly, "come as you are and just be yourself...or the person you would most hope to become."

People walk slowly through the outfield; feeling the simple thrill of the grass under their feet, then stand gazing into the wonder of the cornfield that grows at the back edge of the field. The ghosts of every American's youth are there, after all, and it puts visitors in touch with something real...deep inside.

Americans have always believed that even with two out in the bottom of the 9th, there's still a chance. After all, someone could step up to the plate and belt one out. Or someone could make a shoestring catch to save the game. Who knows? It could happen. After all, things looked bad for the Pilgrims, but they didn't quit. And what about those Patriots back in '76? They were some of the biggest underdogs in history, but they pulled it out, right?

So whether it's by watching 100 years of baseball films on the silver screen, or simply standing alone on the pitcher's mound in Dyersville, Americans seem to connect with the best part of themselves through the game of baseball. As a nation, we believe there's always hope for anyone…if they just hang in there and keep swingin'. And even if they can't win in regulation, there's always extra innings.

"It ain't over till it's over."

Take it from me. When it comes to being an American, forget everything you've heard about the songs of robins being the harbinger of spring. Instead, grab your glove, pull your baseball cap down tight, put your hand to your ear and listen for the *real* song of the season…the call of "Batter Up!"

Lessons From Zen

Strange as it seems, I've been into the teachings of Zen since I was a little boy. No, I'm not talking about sitting cross-legged for decades at a time. I'm talking about Fred Zen, an amazing old guy who lived just up the road from us when I was a kid.

My mom told me Fred was a disreputable old reprobate, which, of course, only made him more irresistible to me and my circle of friends. Fred seemed to know everything worth knowing, and I always admired his simple, down home wisdom.

One Saturday morning, I was sitting in my favorite spot by our local pond. I hardly ever caught any fish there, but I never stopped trying. (I subscribed to the "McElligot's Pool" school of fishing, popularized in the 1947 book by Dr. Seuss, which suggests that just because you've never caught anything in a body of water doesn't mean there isn't anything to catch in there. It's just that you haven't caught it *yet*.)

I'd been sitting for about an hour when I saw Fred approaching the lake. Although he didn't see me, I watched as he stopped in front of a section of lake littered with stumps and submerged logs. He cast his lure into the murky water and within seconds, he was reeling in a fish! He tossed it into a bucket, then turned back to the lake and cast into the tangle of branches and stumps again. Moments later, he had another fish!

Much as I idolized Fred Zen, seeing him catch fish on his first two casts was more than I could stand. I walked over and said, "Hi, Fred."

Fred turned and called back, "Hey, kid! How've ya been doin' over there?"

"Not so good, I afraid. I haven't even had a bite."

"Well, I ain't a bit surprised," Fred said, casually tossing his lure between two ominous-looking logs. Then, without looking back, he asked, "Tell me somethin', kid. Do you like catchin' fish?"

What kind of question was that? Of course I did.

"Well, I figured you must catch a lot of 'em over there, coz that's where you always seem to fish."

"Well, that's not the reason," I confessed. "I like that spot because there's no snags. That way, I never lose any hooks or bobbers."

"Oh," he said, now busy fighting a nice-sized bass. "I s'pose that's true. You ain't gonna lose any tackle over there. But I guess I gotta ya again. Do you like catchin' fish?"

"Yeah," I said, beginning to wonder if the old man had finally lost his mind.

"Well, it just seems to me that if ya wanna to start catchin' fish, yer gonna haveta start fishin' where the fish are."

Still fighting the bass, he said over his shoulder, "If ya wanna get anywhere in this world, I afraid you're gonna haveta lose some tackle sometimes. There ain't no way around it, far as I can see."

Then he turned all the way around and looked me straight in the eye. "You know what I mean, kid?"

Turning back to the water, he added, "If ya just wanna sit on the bank and play it safe, that's fine. But if wanna catch fish, sometimes ya gotta get out there and risk some tackle. And only you can decide what you really wanna get outta the experience—but ya can't have it both ways."

Forty years later, I can still hear Fred's words. And you know, throughout my life, whenever I've wanted something with all my heart, I learned that I have to summon my courage and *go* straight to that place where my dream lies hidden. Then, even if it's scary sometimes, I know I'll have to cast out into the snags—which means that sometimes I'm going to lose some tackle.

But I also know that whether I'm working toward my dream or just sitting on the bank, Fred was right—the choice is still always mine to make.

Amazing Stuff

There's an old adage that says: "empty minds are like empty lots, they both tend to collect junk." I figured I'd prove the truth of that old adage by offering a bunch of what I call "amazing stuff" I've collected in the junkyard of my mind over the years. I love little known things like these, and maybe you can share them at your next party. Then again, if you do, it may be your last invitation to a party, so you might want to give it some thought first.

For starters, did you know that if you took a penny on November 1st, and doubled it every day, by the end of one month you'd have the approximate amount the average college student owes on a student loan at graduation?

Or did you know that if you exceeded the speed of light, you'd actually begin going backward in time? That might come in handy if you're late for an appointment, but it would make it hard to read the traffic signs on the freeway.

In ancient China, doctors were paid when their patients were kept well, and not when they were sick. It makes me wonder how HMO's worked at that time. ("Well, Mr. Jones, I can approve you for three more days of wellness, but then you're going to have to contract pneumonia.")

Here's one I found fascinating, being a musician myself. I was surprised to learn that of all the instruments in the world, the oboe is considered the most difficult to play, especially if you don't use your mouth.

Along those same lines, I read somewhere that Beethoven was totally deaf when he composed his famous Ninth Symphony. When asked by an interviewer how he managed to accomplish it, the composer responded, "Eh? What?"

Here's an idea that could make some enterprising dairy farmer a pile of money. There are more than 50,000 earthquakes in the world in any given year. If he could tap all that energy, a farmer could make milkshakes right inside the cow and eliminate the middleman!

And speaking of inventions, did you know that in 1875 the director of the U.S. Patent Office urged the government to close his department because, as far as he could see, everything worth inventing had been invented already. (It turned out that he was right, of course.)

If you're young and feel like you're getting nowhere, maybe you can take heart from Napoleon. By age 26, he'd already conquered all of Italy—but he still couldn't qualify for a Visa card without a cosigner. While he was pillaging the various countries around him, Napoleon often liked to kick back every now and then and drink a wine cooler. It turns out that one of his favorite drinking vessels was made from the skull of the famous Italian adventurer Cagliostro. (Although that's pretty amazing, history doesn't tell us what Cagliostro thought about that.)

Well, there they are. Just a few examples of what happens to the human mind when a person has WAY too much free time. We'll talk more...

Bob's Hook Shot

During my first year in college, some friends and I were invited to play basketball for a local church team. We'd all played high school ball, so our addition instantly made that team a contender for the Church League title.

One by one, we walked through our opponents, and folks at church began to treat us like celebrities. They told us how much they enjoyed watching us play, and how important it was for them to have us as positive role models for the youngsters in the congregation.

There was only one member of the starting five left from the old team. His name was Bob, and he was a constant source of embarrassment to the rest of us. He was in his mid-30s (ancient, in our eyes) and to put it kindly, Bob was not a gifted athlete. In fact, only bad things seemed to happen every time Bob touched the ball. But he was the church Youth Leader and taught Sunday school, and also, to our chagrin…captain of the team.

Weeks went by. We continued to win game after game, never facing any real competition, until one night, we ran into a team that was also composed of college players. For the first time that season, we found ourselves having to work hard just to stay even.

With 15 seconds left in the game, we actually found ourselves behind by two points. Bob slowly brought the ball up court while the other team dropped back to play half court defense.

Unguarded, Bob dribbled the ball to the center circle. Then he did an amazing thing. He turned his body parallel to the basket and sent a hook shot sailing into the air—from half court!

Needless to say, none of us had expected Bob to throw up a shot like that, so we were in no position to rebound, but it didn't matter. The ball caromed off the rim and sailed out of bounds, untouched. Our opponents threw the ball in, the buzzer sounded, and the game was over.

Back at the bench, we stood in stunned silence, waiting for Bob to say something, but he didn't seem to notice. Finally, one of the guys asked, "What in God's name were you thinking, Bob?"

Wiping his face with a towel, Bob looked over toward the stands and said quietly, "You see those three little kids sitting over there in the bleachers? I promised them at church Sunday that I'd try a hook shot from half court sometime during the game. Since we've been beating everybody so bad, I didn't think it would be a problem. But since the game was so close, I never got the chance. So when I brought the ball up court, I knew that would be the last chance I'd get."

"So what?" somebody asked, voicing the question for all of us.

"Hey, don't you see? I'd made those kids a promise and I had to keep it," Bob said, without hesitation.

At first, I was convinced Bob had lost his mind. But as we stood there, surrounded by people from the church who'd brought their kids to watch us play, I knew Bob was right. In the bigger game—the one that really mattered—there were some things that were more important than winning basketball games...things like keeping promises.

And you know, thirty years later, I can't recall one single other play from that season. And even though we lost that game, I gained something far greater that night, and the memory of Bob's hook shot, and his lesson about keeping promises, has made me a better father, a better lover...and a better man.

What's In A Name?

*I*t isn't easy having a famous name, especially when *you're* not one who made the name famous. I'm not a football fan, but I understand the other Gary Anderson is a pretty good kicker. All I know is that he's made it hard on all the other Gary Andersons in the world, all of us laboring under his shadow, simply because we share the same name.

Unless your name is Ghrouldron Schliebriectman or something to that effect, it's a common problem, having the same name as someone famous. I know a high school girl shackled with the name Hilary Clinton, for instance. But this is my article, so I'll be talking about myself, and all the other Gary Andersons in the world.

Don't get me wrong. I've grown accustomed to running into other Andersons. They're everywhere. My dad's side of the family is from Minnesota, and when people ask me, "Which part of Minnesota?" I say, "It's *Minnesota*...pick a town and there'll be Andersons there, and I'm probably related to every one of them in some way or another."

Just for fun, I once looked in the Minneapolis phone book and counted thirteen pages of Andersons, more than Smith and Jones combined. Last summer, I went fishing on a Minnesota lake with a couple other guys...and two out of the three of us in the boat were named Gary Anderson.

So it goes without saying that there are many other Gary Andersons are out there, and I'll bet if you ask them, they'll all tell you they're tired of being asked their name by someone on the phone and then being asked, "Are you the REAL Gary Anderson?"

Now I ask you, what can a person say to a question like that? There *is* no answer, really. If you say you're not the real Gary Anderson, what does that mean? Are you admitting that you're a *pretend* Gary Anderson, even though you've been Gary Anderson since the day you were born? But if you say yes, the person on the phone instantly says, "I want to tell you, you're a heck of an athlete, man!"

So what does a person do, especially if you happen to be a Gary Anderson who's trying to make a name for himself in some other field, like writing, perhaps? Change your name? After working for more than twenty years to build up name recognition in your field, that doesn't seem like a good option.

Being a humorist, I automatically find myself looking for something to snicker about in the whole mess. I tell myself it could be worse…my name could be Jack the Ripper or Trigger. (Although I suppose the chances are that most folks wouldn't ask, "Wow! Are you the real Trigger?")

Sad as it seems, when all is said and done, the problem may actually be unsolvable. But faced with an unsolvable problem, I can always hear my grandpa's voice echoing in my head, offering sage advice, saying, "Stop your whining and get back to work."

Hmmm…maybe there *is* a solution, after all.

The Black Hole

When I coached volleyball at Duck Hollow High, I used to love away games. They gave our kids a chance to experience the larger world, visit new places—and they were usually safer for everyone concerned.

Modern volleyball players see mostly nice, tight nets and rigid standards in the gyms where they play. The referee stands are carpeted, with ladders and side rails. Most of the schools in our league had those types of set ups, too. But Duck Hollow was a very notable exception. Our net setup barely passed state regulations, due in part to the fact that inspectors were afraid to come to our gym and check it out.

Our standards were made of plumbing pipe, welded together and stuck into cement poured into old tires. (Radial tires; if you please…we did have *some* class!) Our tattered net was held in place by tired ropes that sometimes flew apart with no warning, causing considerable excitement. In fact, our practices were often disrupted by frenzied cries of "Hit the deck!" as net, standards and guide ropes came crashing down around us in wild disarray.

Actually, though, our makeshift setup did give us quite a home court advantage. Throughout the night, our wild-eyed opponents would stand around nervously, afraid to touch anything for fear of causing the whole gym to collapse, which meant they couldn't block or spike (two things that are fairly important to a volleyball team's ultimate success). As a team, we were OK with that, since we needed all the help we could get.

Sometimes, in fact, our whole team was taught to yell, "Hit the deck!" in unison, which would cause our terrified opponents to curl into fetal positions, hoping to survive whatever impending disaster was about to occur. With our opponents so incapacitated, one of our players would gently drop the ball into their court for a side out. In fact, we actually listed that tactic as #7 in our playbook. (Play #8 was yelling, "Hit the deck!" IN EARNEST while our equipment melted around us like matter being sucked down a black hole, which is how our gym's nickname—the Black Hole—came into being.)

In order for the person unlucky enough to be forced by the league to serve as the "up official" at one of our home games, they first had to step onto a kindergarten chair, which served as our version of a ladder, and then onto a table—which passed for our referee stand. Once on the table, the official had to hold onto the net standard for balance, which meant that whenever the net came tumbling down, the standards went with it—usually bringing the official along for the ride—and went rolling in crazy radial tire-and-cement circles on the ground. Although it could be exciting, few officials seemed interested in taking advantage of the experience.

With a setup like that, our referees had to be agile and alert if they were to survive. In fact, you could easily pick out the officials who had worked Duck Hollow games at tournament time, because they seemed to develop various nervous ticks and twitches. And needless to say, everyone knew it wasn't safe to yell, "Hit the deck" around them!

Another way our gym lived up to its nickname was in our lighting—or lack of it. There were times when volleyballs simply disappeared overhead. Opposing hitters would approach the net and then stand there, waiting, with no idea of when, where, or even if the ball was ever going to come down.

That situation did make for some pretty funny moments, though. I once saw an opposing middle hitter hover in midair for over ten seconds just by waving her arms. The sheer force of her spiking motion kept her aloft, arms flailing like helicopter blades. Although it was an impressive display, I think she hurt herself in the end, because her coach had to take her out. (Although, to be fair, it may have been from emotional strain—the poor girl was crying so hard at the time it I couldn't tell. But it didn't matter. We just chalked her up as another victim of the Black Hole.)

In the end, I must admit that playing home games in a place like the Black Hole was an entertaining, even if somewhat dangerous, experience. I'm willing to bet that none of our players will ever forget it—some of them still have scars to remind them. But I sometimes wonder if any of them ever get as nostalgic about that old gym as I do.

After all, just thinking about the old Black Hole brings back memories. Of course, so does thinking about my first root canal.

The Entrepreneurs

One of the ladies at our local grocery store leaned across the counter last week and asked me, "I have just one question for you. How much of the stuff you write is actually true?"

I had to laugh and say, "Well, not much, I'm afraid. If it were all true, I'd have the most bizarre life in the world."

But last night, my daughter was working on an assignment for a class, in which she was supposed to list her father's previous occupations. By the time we'd finished, her list featured 32 different jobs I'd held, however briefly, over the course of my lifetime. And with a background like that, I couldn't help but collect a few episodes that were not only true, but fairly strange, as well. Here's a few examples, and I swear every one is true—more or less—take your pick of which ones you want to believe.

You see, I've been an entrepreneur pretty much all my life, and with the help of my younger brother, Scooter, tried a number of mail order schemes in our younger days, all in an attempt to cash in on the big money we'd always heard about. Our first attempt was something we called an "Emergency Smoke Kit." It consisted of a cigarette encased in a glass cylinder, bearing the message, "In Case of Emergency, Break Glass." We took out ads in several national magazines, spent thousands of dollars—and sold exactly seven kits. But we weren't discouraged. The fact that we'd sold *any* told us it was at least possible to make money in mail order. The key seemed to be coming up with just the right product—that gadget that would make us rich beyond our wildest imaginations.

So we came up with a new product: a pendant bearing a reproduction of a star map, to be worn around the neck in case a person happened to be abducted by aliens. We called it "The Close Encounter Pendant," and found a company in China willing to make it for us. The map featured on the pendant had originally been drawn by a woman who'd been abducted by aliens. She'd apparently seen it on the wall of the waiting room inside the spaceship while she was waiting for her number to be called.

Our target audience was folks who were about to be abducted by a group of aliens who had gotten lost somehow. Once the aliens saw the pendant you were wearing, they'd know that not only did you know where they were from, but you had a hip sense of fashion, as well. Then, after a little small talk and maybe some sun tea, you could offer to let the aliens borrow your pendant so they could find their way back home without having to suffer further embarrassment by having to stop and ask anybody else for directions.

It was a cool product, and this time we took out ads in various UFO magazines. To our surprise, we received orders from around the world, including a number of people who told us about their own abduction experiences in great detail—encounters during which their mental processes had apparently failed to survive.

Still, we didn't care where they were from, or whether their letters should have been written in crayon. If a person sent $14.95 (plus $5.00 shipping and handling), and included an Earth-based zip code, we sent them a pendant.

In retrospect, I suppose the worst thing about our encounter pendant venture was that we actually made a little money from the deal. If we would have lost our proverbial shirts, we might have quit, right there and then. But now we had proof it was possible for even the most hair-brained invention to put some money in our pockets, which made us more determined than ever to find that Big Idea.

We're still looking. For instance, since anti-aging creams will always be big business, I toyed with inventing a potion I called Oil of Oleo, and to my amazement, it actually *did* make me look younger...about 15 minutes younger.

However the side effects made it a bit impractical. Every time I put it on before retiring, I kept sliding out of bed. But I was determined to follow this through. I came up with a second substance I called "Scruffer," which was specifically designed to counteract the slipperiness of Oil of Oleo. And it worked! The only trouble was that an application of Scruffer made me look 15 minutes *older*, so the two substances canceled each other out.

But I promise you one thing: I don't give up easily, and a person never knows when that one great Big Idea will finally strike, whether it has to do with emergency cravings, lost aliens or sliding out of bed in the middle of the night.

My Year As A Tackling Dummy

I spent one year in organized football…my freshman year in high school. I weighed 130 pounds, if that, but I wanted to get the most out of my high school experience, and football was the first sport of the year. So I signed up, put on a practice uniform (which weighed almost as much as I did) and trotted out onto the playing field.

Our coach, a stern, grim-faced guy who scared the life out of me from the moment he looked at me, ordered everybody to line up in the spots they wanted to play. Being a polite kid, I found a line that didn't have too many guys in it and joined that one. I figured the competition would be less that way, and I was right, but hadn't given any thought to WHY that line might have been so short.

It turned out the line I'd picked was for players who wanted to be tackles. *Tackles.* Tackles are big guys, mean guys, guys who strike fear in the hearts of opposing players by their sheer size and nasty attitude—guys who'd rather knock people down than have to worry about mundane things like catching or carrying the football. Guys who lived only for the opportunity to dish out pain and suffering.

But like I said, I weighed 130 pounds, and as I looked around, I found my eyes looking directly into the midsections of most of the other guys in the line. Those guys were BIG and they were tall. But I was so overwhelmed by the entire experience of being on a football field for the first time in my life that I didn't realize the magnitude of my mistake until the team began to practice for real.

The coach announced that we were about to run a drill called "the Alley." I'd heard about alleys, and the little town where I grew up actually had a couple alleys, but they were just little dirt paths that kids used as shortcuts between people's houses, so I didn't realize how dangerous alleys could really be!

I was about to find out.

"Anderson!" the coach bellowed. "You start!"

I dutifully went and stood at one end of the Alley, quaking in my cleats, while another player, whose shoulders were so wide they blocked out the sun, stood at the other. He looked as if he'd just been paroled from prison, possibly on a manslaughter charge. Still, he seemed like a nice enough guy...that is, until he strapped his helmet on. Then his face distorted into some sort of hideous monstrosity, and his main goal in life seemed to be to destroy whoever or whatever got in his way. Unfortunately, the only thing standing in his way at that particular moment was me!

I began to worry—but I didn't have time to worry long.

The coach barked a signal and handed a football to the guy, who instantly came charging straight ahead. His head was down, his legs were pumping, his cleats throwing up divots of sod behind him as he churned toward me. Instinctively, I took a step back, which proved to be a mistake for several reasons.

First, the guy barreled into me such force that I was lifted into the air, becoming airborne long enough to wonder if I'd been sent into orbit. Second, even as I was on my way back to Earth, I could hear the coach bellowing at me, letting me know that not only had I disgraced myself and every male of the human species since the birth of Adam, but also that I'd have to do the whole thing *again*.

Although I was a little sorry about disgracing Adam and his descendants, I had absolutely NO desire to participate in the Alley again. But as I turned to retreat, a crowd of other players gathered around me, barring me from escape. Instead, I found myself shoved back into position at one end of the Alley while another player, this one even bigger than the last, stood waiting at the other.

There was no doubt about it. The game of football was rapidly losing its appeal to me—and I'd only been out for fifteen minutes. As I stood there trying to collect my wits, I saw the coach hand a ball to the new guy and shout, "Go!"

Instantly, the new runner barreled toward me, a look of grim determination on his face. Again, I took a step back. Although I knew it was a mistake, I just couldn't help myself. I should have predicted the outcome. As the runner hit me squarely in the chest with his helmet, I went sprawling onto my back, digging a long trench with my shoulder pads as I skidded along the ground. Then he ran over the top of me, stepping on me several times as he sprinted out the other end of the Alley.

As I pulled myself off the turf and began examining my body for cleat marks, the coach was screaming something in my ear, but to be honest, I didn't hear a lot of what he was saying. Everything seemed to be echoing, as if all the grey matter inside my head had been removed, leaving nothing but an empty cavity. I uttered a silent prayer, thanking God that most of my body parts still seemed to be attached, although several of them now appeared to be in different locations than they'd been a few moments ago.

In the midst of my pain and confusion, I learned one of life's most painful lessons at that moment. If you don't win the Alley confrontation, you have to keep doing it—again and again—until either you finally do win, or they carry your lifeless body from the field. Either way, it didn't seem like much of a choice.

Meanwhile, the coach's face was turning the most amazing shade of purple, and the veins in his neck bulged as he screamed obscenities into the ear hole of my helmet. For a moment, I had a brief hope that maybe he'd explode—or have a heart attack and die right there on the spot. But although the idea had promise, it didn't happen, and I knew I'd have to have another go at the Alley.

Resigning myself to my fate, I lined up at the end of the Alley. But this time, I was determined to put up a scrap—or die trying. Wait a minute! What was I saying?

I didn't have time to debate about whether or not I had truly lost my sanity. The coach lined up a third runner at the other end of the Alley and screamed, "Now, Anderson, don't you let him get past you again, you understand!"

I shook my head. Although my mind was reeling, all I knew at that moment was that I had no desire whatsoever to spend the rest my life being mugged in that Alley, so with grim determination, I squatted down, gritted my teeth and dug my cleats deep into the turf.

At the coach's signal, the ball carrier rushed at me, nostrils flaring, growling like some crazed animal. I closed my eyes and flung myself forward to meet the runner head-on. The power of the collision sent us both reeling. I remember hearing a sickening thud, briefly seeing stars, but then everything went black.

I have no idea how long I was out. All I know is that when I came to, I was laying on my back, looking up toward the sky—a position that, although I didn't know it at the time, I would come to perfect as the season went on. I was surrounded by a group of helmeted teammates, all staring down at me.

Through the haze, I heard someone say, "Anderson! Hey! Are you OK?"

As I tried to speak, the words seemed to be coming from somewhere far away. After a few moments, I heard what seemed to be my voice saying, "I think so. Where am I?"

(I know—it was a trite cliché, but it's hard to be witty when you've just had all your senses knocked into the next time zone.)

Another faraway voice said, "No really, man. Are you all right?"

I shook my head, trying to remember who I was, and finally said, "I don't know. Am I dead?"

Amid gales of laughter, I heard somebody say, "No."

Lifting myself onto one elbow, I said, "Oh, good. Then I'm already doing better than I thought."

That first day of football practice was the longest day of my life. By the time it was over, I had learned hundreds of new places where a human body can be sprained, pulled, torn, bruised, and mutilated. (I didn't know it then, but I would add even more entries to that list as the season progressed.)

I spent the entire season on the injured reserve list. In fact, my mom got so tired of writing notes describing my various injuries that she finally created a generic form, listing about two hundred problem areas. Then each day, all she had to do was to check off whatever was my *injury du jour*, which saved her a bunch of time and energy.

As the season wore on, I made a pact with myself that if by some miracle I managed to survive the year, I'd never go out for football again. I promised myself that if I could just hang in there and complete the season, I'd watch football from a safe distance for the rest of my life—say, the length of a living room, on television.

Then, one day, an amazing thing happened. I was well enough to play, even though I was fifth string. We were playing a team from a school I'd never heard of, and we were winning 56-0 in the fourth quarter.

Amazingly, the coach bellowed my name, saying, "Anderson, go in for Hannigan!"

I was stunned. That had never happened before! But I quickly put on my helmet, ran onto the field and took my place at offensive tackle. The defensive lineman directly across from me looked old enough to be my father. He had a three-day growth of beard, and held the stub of a cigar between his green teeth.

I was too scared to look him in the eye. I took up my three-point stance as our quarterback barked out signals. Then I surged forward, and launched my body into the monster in front of me. It was like running into a fence post. Instantly, I could feel various parts of my anatomy begin to crumble into dust. Then I felt myself being lifted into the air and I came down some five yards from the point where I had started.

I spent the rest of the game on my back, but mercifully, it was the final quarter, so there wasn't much of the game left. After a few plays, it became the most natural thing in the world to have my body become airborne and then land with a thud. I eventually learned how to land on my back without having every trace of wind knocked out of me, and I could almost make it back to the huddle before everyone else was moving back toward the line for the next play. It didn't matter—hey, I was finally in the game, and that was what really counted!

It was lucky for me that I had enjoyed that playing time, because I didn't get in many other games after that. (If we weren't either ahead or behind by 50 points, I knew I wouldn't see much action, anyway, so I wasn't too surprised.)

But in the final game of the season, another miracle happened! I found myself in the right tackle position, squatting in my three-point stance, again listening to the quarterback bark out signals. When I heard him say, "Hike!" I surged forward, and instead of finding myself flying through the air, the kid in front of me fell onto *his* back!

I was confused, and for a moment, I couldn't comprehend what had happened. Instinctively, I reached out my hand to help him up, and said, "Sorry."

He looked up at me and said, "Oh, that's OK. I'm used to it."

It was an amazing thing! For the first time in my life, I'd finally met someone with whom I could identify as a football player! A kid who knew what it was like to spend all afternoon either airborne or on his back. From that play on, I pushed that kid backwards and then helped him up on every offensive play. (But I'll tell you a secret: I never hit him hard enough to hurt him. After all, I knew what it was like to get pushed around like that, and I couldn't see any reason to maim the poor kid.)

When the game was over, I sought that kid out, shook his hand and thanked him. He looked at me like I was out of my mind, but I didn't care. I knew I owed him a great debt, though he'd never know about it. After all, the football season was finally OVER, and I had not only survived, but I'd actually managed to push ONE kid around for most of an afternoon. I'd accomplished more than what I'd set out to do, and now, I'd *never* have to put on those pads again!

I walked off the field and never looked back.

Over the years, people have asked me if I'd do it again if I got the chance. When I hear that question, I think about it for a couple seconds, then smile and say, "Well, let me put it this way. Since that day, not only have I *not* played football, but I've also never even been tempted to walk through another alley!"

Opal's Cheater's Quilt

Being fairly new to my newly adopted rural Midwestern area, I'm still fascinated by the folks around me. Although they find me a bit odd, I have a suspicion that my neighbors are secretly glad to have someone around who hasn't heard all their stories a hundred times over. That arrangement works well for me, too, because I'm perfectly content to mine this rich new vein of stories I've discovered.

For instance, last week I paid a visit to Opal Endersen, my neighbor just down the road. (That's not her real name, of course. She's a lovely, proud woman in her 80s, and I know she'd be mortified if anyone learned the "secret" I'm about to reveal.)

As I walked in Opal's front door, I was greeted by a large piece of patterned cloth stretched across a quilting rack in the living room. When I commented on it, I could see Opal's blue eyes begin to twinkle.

"It's great to see that folks around here still make quilts," I said. "That's one reason I love this area. Old-timey things like this still go on."

Opal just smiled. I imagined she was remembering a time when quilt making wasn't considered such an "old-timey" activity.

We sat for a time in silence, both looking at the quilt. When she finally spoke, there was a touch of wistfulness in Opal's voice. "When I was young, all the neighbors used to get together and make quilts. And even today, my sisters and granddaughter still come and help me sometimes. But now, I mostly do it myself. This one's for my grandson. He's away at college, and I guess he wants something to remember me by when…I'm gone."

If you know any Midwesterners, especially older Midwesterners, you know that they're a self-deprecating lot, and they usually don't take praise well. So when I told Opal I thought that was a wonderful thing to do for her grandson, she just replied, "Well, it's really only a cheater's quilt."

I'd never heard the term before. "I don't understand," I said. "What do you mean, 'cheater's quilt'?"

Opal aimed a frail finger toward the quilting frame. "You see the pattern in the fabric? It looks just like quilts you would have seen back in the late 1800s, right?"

I nodded, though I'm definitely no expert on 19th century quilt patterns.

"Well, if I was making a real quilt, I would have hand-cut each individual piece and then sewn them all together, one-by-one. But as it is, I'm just hand-stitching around a printed pattern on one large piece of cloth, which makes it look like the pieces actually were stitched together, you see?"

I did understand what Opal was saying, but there was something about it that bothered me. I could picture Opal, sitting at her quilting rack for what had to have been dozens of hours, hand stitching around the pattern. Somehow, it just didn't seem right to refer to all that loving effort as "cheating."

But there was no such doubt in Opal's mind: she knew perfectly well what went into making a "real" quilt, and since she was taking a shortcut, she was "cheating." Period. End of discussion.

Using Opal's yardstick, I could think of a thousand modern things that should be labeled "cheater's merchandise." I also thought about the consumers who gladly buy that merchandise, either because they can't find quality alternatives, or even sadder, because they no longer know any better. Somehow, I just couldn't allow Opal's hand-stitched gift of love to be compared to that type of junk. But no matter which tack I tried, Opal was unmoved, and in the end I gave up, because deep down, where the truth is, I knew exactly what she was saying—and I couldn't disagree.

So we again sat in silence for what seemed like a long while, then I got up, we said our goodbyes, and I walked toward the door. But as I left, I took a last look at the quilt, wondering how many nights that sweet lady had spent alone at that frame, her fingers sewing endless tiny stitches into her grandson's quilt. Surely that had to count for something.

I thanked Opal for the conversation and cookies, and started for home. But I tumbled the whole conversation over in my mind, again and again, as I walked slowly down the dusty gravel road.

She'd been right, of course. Opal knew it, and so did I. It really doesn't matter what our mass-produced society would have us believe. Somewhere deep inside, we all instinctively know real quality when we see it, and putting anything less than our best into whatever we do *is* cheating…whether we're creating a quilt—or a world.

Quantum Fishin'

There are many mysteries in our universe that have baffled scientists from the dawn of time...odd quirks of nature that have defied our understanding from the first moment men began to think about something other than simply how to scrounge up their next dinoburger. And although it certainly qualifies as one of those infinite mysteries, I'm not talking about trying to refold a road map while driving. What I'm talking about is the field of quantum mechanics.

Ever since their introduction by physicists, the theories and principles of the quantum world have proven to be nearly impossible for the average person to comprehend...that is, unless you happen to be a fisherman. Whether they knew it or not, fishermen have been using quantum principles since the dawn of time.

Here's an example: one of the earliest quantum theories was proposed by Albert Einstein. He called it the Theory of Relativity. Even today, most people don't have a clue as to how it works. Yet the Theory of Relativity is a piece of cake to fishermen. All they have to do is compare an hour spent beside a slow moving river, watching the water gently rolling by, a fish biting every few minutes, to a similar amount of time spent trying to fish with two cranky kids, one whining that she wants to go home and the other relieving his boredom by chucking rocks into the water, right next to your bobber. Nobody needs to explain the meaning of Relativity to a fisherman.

Another problem with quantum physics is its strange terminology. It features bizarre things with names like quarks, leptons, and mesons. But though they may be totally alien concepts to the average person, those terms don't even faze a fisherman. When you mention a lepton or meson to a fisherman, he'll tell you those are simply the brand names of lures designed to catch walleye or northern pike on a Minnesota lake.

A theory that has gained a great deal of attention in recent years has been dubbed the Chaos Theory. It's a wildly complicated concept to most people, but perfectly understood by any angler who has ever taken a group of six-year-olds on an overnight fishing trip.

There's also a generally accepted belief among quantum physicists that the point of view of the observer influences the outcome of any experiment. In other words, the theory proposes that simply observing an experiment will have an effect on the outcome of that experiment, and observers in different locations will obtain different results, based upon their points of view. Now I admit, that idea is a little harder to explain than the first couple we've discussed, but perhaps I can shed some light on the subject by describing a fishing trip I recently took with my friend, Spider McGee.

We were trolling on Lost Lake, with no success. (In fairness, I don't know if that was the name of the lake or not. As usual, we had no idea where we were at the time, and stumbled across this pretty lake. So the name Lost Lake seemed as good as any, and seemed especially apropos at the time.)

In honor of the new lake, we both decided to try a new lure…a #2 Lepton, if memory serves. We rigged our lines in exactly the same way and then cast our lures into Lost Lake at exactly same moment. After two hours of experimentation, I'd caught nothing. Spider, on the other hand, had hauled in a five-pound northern and three good-sized walleyes. (To be fair, he'd also caught 14 crappies, 5 bass, a dozen perch and a couple hundred bluegills, but I refused to count those, because we'd both agreed that Leptons were specifically designed to catch northerns.)

It was easy to see that the results of our experiment would completely different, depending on which one of us you happened to talk to when we pulled our boat back up to the dock at the end of the day. Spider was ecstatic, but I was grumpy for two days. If you also look at the experiment from the Theory of Relativity point of view, Spider would have said the three hours we spent on the lake seemed to fly by. But you'd asked me, the afternoon was slightly longer than the last Ice Age. As the day wore on, I even managed to slip in a little coursework in Chaos, having to work my way through a backlash that made the Gordian Knot look like a pile of jumbo Tinker Toys.

As you can see from that example, one fishing excursion can easily involve a number of different quantum principles. But as it turned out, we were just beginning our journey into the quantum world when we finished our actual fishing. Once we got back to the dock, we learned about the quantum concept of the "supercollider." (That's the devices physicists use to study mesons, quarks and all their weird cousins.) As we neared the dock, a wind began whipping the water into foam, and I suddenly I found my boat had become a supercollider, smashing not only into the dock and four other boats, but also into my trailer as we struggled to load it up.

(A useful aside here: perhaps you may have heard that congress has been authorized some $600 billion or so to build a supercollider in some remote area of the country. But if you happen to have a congressman as a fishing buddy, I'd appreciate it if you'd mention that I'd be more than willing to sell my own personal supercollider to the government for less than *half* that...and I'll throw the trailer in *free*. I figure it's the least I can do for my country.)

So you can see that fishermen have been in tune with the fundamentals of quantum physics from the very beginning, whether they knew it or not. And although they never realized it, they rely on quantum principles every time they attempt to stuff a tackle box with three times more equipment than it was originally designed to hold. They employ the quantum theory every time they magically transform one tiny fish into a large number of *big* fish while describing a weekend excursion to their friends. They use the Theory of Relativity every time they stretch "one last cast" into an hour's worth of fishing at the end of the day. The list goes on and on, and yet no one has ever given fishermen the credit they deserve for their innate understanding of the quantum universe.

So, the next time you're seeking answers to your questions on quantum mechanics, don't spend hours trying to track down a physicist—everybody knows they're notoriously hard to find. (After all, it's common knowledge that there never seems to be a physicist around when you really need one.) Instead, just go find yourself a fisherman—they're *everywhere*. (In fact, there are times when you can't swing a cat around in a room without hitting a dozen or more.)

Once you've found your fishermen, the chances are good that they'll be glad to tell you more than you ever wanted to know about the subject—way, way more, in fact, because fishing stories do have a tendency to go on…and on…and on.

But while you're waiting for your fisherman to wind down, you'll also be gaining some valuable insights into another difficult and mysterious segment of the quantum universe…the concept of eternity.

I'd go into that, but I can't right now. I still have a huge Quantum Backlash to unravel.

More Amazing Stuff

I've uncovered many strange and unusual facts over the course of my life. In fairness, it's not really the facts themselves that are so remarkable. The truly remarkable thing is that a person would bother to remember them at all.

My friends have told me it means I have *way* too much time on my hands. But I can't help it. Some things just stick in a person's mind, whether you like it or not. I mean; have you ever tried to decide what you remember and what you don't? Be honest: it's not that easy, is it?

So in the next few pages I'll be offering some more amazing stuff, and maybe writing it down will help me let it go. Then, if it sticks in *your* mind after that, I'm sorry. So be warned: from this moment, you're on your own.

For starters, did you know that it's almost impossible for the average person to get a feel for the concept of eternity? There is one way you can come close to understanding it, though, and that is while listening to a four-year-old telling you about the latest episode of a sci-fi cartoon they just watched.

Here's one that hits home for me personally. Did you know that if I had started calculating the very second I was born and had continued calculating non-stop until the moment you read these words, I still wouldn't be able to balance my check book?

In the "I'll never get credit for that" department: I can claim the discovery of black holes, long before they were supposedly discovered by astronomers. I could have saved them a great deal of trouble by simply letting them get a look at my college social calendar on any given Saturday night.

Here's a kind of sad one. In 1970, a man named Frankby Irvin paid $20,000 for a single glass paperweight at auction. I know. That would be sad enough, but poor Mr. Irvin also had to pay another $30,000 for therapy after he dropped his new glass paperweight on the way out the door that night.

Did you know that an American dollar bill can only be folded over itself six times? That's the accepted figure, but I managed to fold one seven times once: by putting it in a vise. Still, I suppose most folks don't generally put their dollar bills in a vise, so I guess the six figure is probably as acceptable as any. I also don't recommend the vise method for a more practical reason: store clerks tend to get a little testy when they are handed dollar bills squashed down to the size of dimes.

If you ever get restless while waiting for someone who has insisted on dragging drag out a version of "The Star Spangled Banner" before your favorite sporting event, imagine how the Greeks must feel. Their national anthem has 158 verses! I guess it's lucky for just about everyone involved that they don't win that many Olympic events.

Did you know that no one knows where Mozart is buried? It may sound unbelievable, but no one knows where the body of Voltaire is, either. I don't think it was the same person in charge of both burials, and it may have been an honest mistake, but there just seems to be some carelessness involved there. If anybody knows anything about that, you might tell the proper authorities, because I imagine they're still wondering about it.

Back in 1975, the city fathers of Quebec, Canada, put out $10,000 (Canadian…which is about four dollars American) to build a birdhouse. And more incredibly, did you know that even today, that birdhouse remains vacant? It seems no bird in the entire city could ever come up with the first and last month's rent.

And finally, here's a little known fact that could have changed history. Did you realize that the ancient Egyptians actually slept on pillows made of stone? Just think about it. If they'd slept on regular pillows, they wouldn't have drawn all those pictures on their palace walls of people walking around with stiff necks. Our entire image of the ancient Egyptians would be different today.

Well, there you have it: my latest batch of amazing stuff. If you can use any of it, fine. You're welcome to use it any way you want. But remember, if it sticks in your mind like it has in mine, I tried to warn you in advance!

The Cold (Tablet) War

People say, "Write about what you know," so I find myself writing lots of stories about being lost, and nearly as many about my difficulty with machines and opening packages. Over the years, I've tackled packages of all sorts, from the unsolvable puzzle of opening a pack of graham crackers to the dilemma of not *wanting* to open a Christmas present and spoil the magic.

This time, my nemesis was a pack of cold capsules.

If you've ever had to resort to taking cold capsules during the flu season, you learned several things very quickly: 1) The pills come attached to a piece of light cardboard, each sealed in a little plastic bubble and covered by an aluminum layer; 2) You have to remove a capsule from that "Easy Open" arrangement in order to take it and begin feeling better; 3) You must accomplish this task while your nose is plugged, your head feels like it's full of cotton, your eyes bleary, and wishing you could be experiencing a ten-day out-of-body experience; and 4) Removing a capsule while in your debilitating condition is only slightly less difficult than your run-of-the-mill brain surgery.

Well, that was the situation I was faced with one day last week. I approached the bathroom medicine cabinet with trepidation. Since I have difficulty opening packages when I'm feeling 100%, I knew this would be a special challenge. (I may be a klutz, but at least I'm honest with myself.)

I pulled out a package of cold capsules and tried to tear off one of the little metal tabs…you know, the ones that the company touts as "Easy Open" in huge letters on the front of the package. ("Easy Open." My favorite phrase in the whole world, right behind the phrase "You can't miss it" people always use when they give directions. I always take that last phrase as a personal challenge. Don't you tell *me* I can't miss it! You just watch me! I'll not only miss it, but I'll miss it from several directions, then I'll start all over and miss it again, just to prove it wasn't a fluke the first time!)

I pried up on the tab, and it broke off. Of course…I would have expected nothing less. I cursed under my breath, I pounded my fist on the counter, I shook my head, but I can't say it helped much. In fact, all that effort made my head start spinning worse than before. So I collected myself and came up with Plan B.

Standing next to the toilet, where the light was better, I took a small pair of scissors and carefully sliced the little plastic bubble surrounding the cold pill. To my joy, the pill popped out. But I had only an instant to enjoy my victory. The pill tumbled out of the container hand and dropped into the toilet.

I had to laugh. It seemed like such a perfect metaphor for the entire situation, especially give the way I felt already. But now I was faced with a dilemma. I had just worked like crazy to get that pill out of its "Easy Open" package. I felt so horrible that I didn't think I wanted to go through that entire process again.

But there was a principle involved here. (I was too groggy to know exactly what that principle *was*, but I just knew there was a principle in there somewhere.)

Should I fish the pill out of the toilet or not? I'd won a small victory over the evil "Easy Open" factions of the world already…those folks who take delight in telling their unwitting customers that they can open their packages with little or no effort, and then make those packages impervious to anything but a small grenade.

I pondered my situation. It was the middle of the night. My kids were asleep. No one would ever know if I fished the pill out. (And, of course, you'll never tell anybody, will you?)

I stood looking at the capsule, sitting at the bottom of the bowl, knowing that even though the capsule was designed to dissolve slowly, it wasn't going to remain in capsule form indefinitely. I had to make a decision.

With a sigh, I reached into the toilet and retrieved the capsule. Then, I turned to the sink, and held the capsule under the faucet. The difficult part was done. Now all I had to do was wash off the pill and get it into my system. But the instant the water hit it, the capsule disintegrated in my fingers. There wasn't even enough left to lick off my fingers...not that *that* sounded like a reasonable possibility at that moment, even to my stuffy brain (although, to be honest, I must admit the thought did briefly cross my mind).

I decided to drop that problem, since the disintegration of that pill had created a new dilemma. There were still six more capsules in the package, but as a frugal person, I was greatly bothered by the fact that I'd just wasted one. The question now was: should I take another one? After all, there was another principle involved here! (And just like the last one, I wasn't sure what it was, but principles are principles, right?)

My first instinct said, "No way will I take another pill now!" But my head was throbbing, my eyes hurt, and I wasn't just feeling like something that the cat had dragged in—it was more like something the cat had half-eaten and then forgotten under the refrigerator for several weeks.

I stood there in the middle of the night, thinking...

What did I do, you ask? Well, let me put it this way: if you think it was an easy decision for a Midwesterner to make, think again.

Small Towns—Not Small People

When I began planning my little family's escape from the West Coast to the Midwest, I remember wondering what the folks were going to be like in our new area. There was no shortage of doomsayers among my friends and family, eager to tell me that I was about to leave behind all vestiges of intelligent conversation and culture when I moved to what everyone back there considered the hinterlands.

Well, I must admit that, in spite of all the gloom and doom warnings to the contrary, I have been pleased to discover that the people in our newly adopted home in the Heartland have surprised me beyond my wildest expectations. In fact, not only are they some of the sharpest cookies I've ever encountered, but they sometimes actually make me like I'm a backwoods hillbilly by comparison!

But sometimes, it's hard to find a job in this rural area that is anywhere near what they trained to become, which means the folks around here are often forced to improvise.

For instance, there's a guy in town named Jerry—a man with an extensive physics background. What does he do for a living? He repairs cars at the local car dealership. This guy can explain the intricacies of the chaos theory and then go to tell you exactly how supercolliders work. (And by supercolliders, I'm not talking about the unfortunate results of an auto mishap during Driver's Ed at the local high school—I mean, the real thing!) In fact, Jerry is so knowledgeable in physics that folks for miles around jokingly call him our local "quantum mechanic."

Since high tech jobs are relatively scarce in the area (read: "nonexistent") a number of other folks have taken jobs for which they are seriously overqualified, too. For example, we have a Fine Arts graduate who now paints cars for the county insurance adjuster. There's a Speech major who sells various kinds of brushes door-to-door. An ex-particle physicist now sells particle *board* at our local lumberyard for farmers to use in building new hog confinement buildings.

Sometimes these people and their jobs can make for some pretty strange paradoxes. For instance, there's the Physical Education major who now works in the local furniture store. "It's a living," he says stoically, although I can only imagine how much it must kill him every time he sells a recliner with a built-in remote control, refrigerator and wet bar.

The next town over has an ex-microbiologist who now owns a mini-golf course. When you ask him about it, he just smiles and says, "At least it's small."

A graduate of a Culinary Arts institute now manages the local hamburger stand. In typical "aw, shucks" small-town fashion, she asks, "Hey, it's still food, right?"

The list goes on and on. But those are just a few of the many kinds of trade-offs that folks are willing to make for the privilege of living in this beautiful area—a place where our kids are safe, the schools are good and life is more manageable than in the Big City.

So if you've got a great education, but find yourself living in a place where the hustle and bustle, crime and congestion are threatening to overwhelm you, I can tell you one thing from my own personal experience: don't despair. Even though it may not seem possible at first, the chances are good that you'll be able to find something that is at least remotely connected to your field of expertise once you arrive in the middle of this wonderful land of relative peace and tranquility.

And even if you can't find something that's an exact match for your particular field, you can still take heart. I'll bet you can probably find something just as fulfilling in some other field.

After all, fields are one thing we've got plenty of!

Family Pirate Stories

No matter who you are or where you live, no matter what your family's national origin may be or its social status, I know a little about you…and your family. Now don't get all excited. I haven't gone on the Internet and copied off all your credit card numbers. Those things I know, I know because they're pretty much the same for every person—and every family.

The first thing I know is that every family has certain stories that are generally known only to the members of the immediate family…and even some of those members are kept in the dark. The second thing is that you, as an individual member of your family, are probably embarrassed by some of those stories.

If I've hit the nail on the head with regard to your family, don't fret. All families share that common characteristic. And the reason it happens is simply because people are people—and people come in a wide variety of stripes. The more colorful people a family has contained over the generations, the more interesting the stories that need to be kept from the general public. That just comes with the territory. And whether you like it or not, there's really nothing you can do about having colorful ancestors. If it helps at all, you might try considering them as merely brightly colored foliage on the old family tree.

My own family was no exception to that rule, but as a writer, I was happy about that, since I've always been attracted to the really juicy stories about people I'm related to, past and present—no matter how obscure. My search for interesting ancestors has sometimes meant having to dig up some very old skeletons...I became a family archeologist, if you will, digging up the past.

For instance, when I was just a little guy, my mom let it slip one morning that one of our ancestors had been a pirate! Although she'd never thought about it and she'd only mentioned it in casual conversation, to an eight-year-old, having a real pirate among the branches of our family tree was about as cool as it could get!

There were so many questions swirling through my mind, I didn't know where to begin. For one thing, there was the mystery of how that poor sailing man had managed to get himself sandwiched in among generation after generation of farmers on both sides of our family. After all, as far as I knew, both sides of the family had always lived in the Midwest—2000 miles from the nearest ocean. What could have prompted that lone individual to one day throw down reins to the plow and take off to pursue a life on the high seas? Did he ever sail with anyone famous? And most importantly, had he hidden any treasure and then stashed his maps among all the old letters in my grandma's attic?

I couldn't help myself. I was on fire with the sheer romance of it all. Those were only a few of the things that sent my mind soaring on wild flights of speculation and wonder. And though I never found the answers to most of my questions or discovered a treasure map, it was still a wondrous thing to have such an amazing person hiding among the branches of our mundane family tree—like finding a lone camellia hiding among the branches of a lilac bush.

Another interesting thing I discovered as I grew older and began to become more aware of what was going on was that I also uncovered several other family members who technically might have been thought of as pirates in some circles—and better yet, some of them were still alive. It didn't matter that those folks had never set foot on the deck of a ship, and probably never would. Given the definition of a pirate I was using in my research, those folks qualified.

But making those discoveries quickly led me to another important lesson in life: although most families believe that having a pirate on your family tree is fine, it's only acceptable if that person had plied his trade several generations ago—the farther back, the better.

Here's what I mean: if you call someone's dad or grandfather a thief, that person will tend to get upset. Yet those same people will proudly lay claim to a pirate ancestor who terrorized the Caribbean back in the 1700s, even though that ancestor's activities were hardly distinguishable from those being carried on by members of the current generation.

Although it was a source of frustration for me, I finally had to hush up everything I knew about the current crop of pirates in our family, since it would probably cause my relatives considerable embarrassment if it became general knowledge. But I couldn't help thinking about another eight-year-old boy in some future generation, studying a picture of our family tree and then hearing his mother point out this current crowd of pirates and exclaiming, "Now that bunch! My goodness, son, they were really something else!"

Would that mother of the future use the word "pirate" to describe those people? Will those same people I wasn't even permitted to mention during my own lifetime suddenly become cool to that future young boy after a couple generations have gone by? Although I'll never know for sure, I know which way I'd bet if given the choice.

And finally, here's other funny thing: as I grow older, I've found that pirates don't seem to interest me as much as they did when I was a kid. I guess pirates sort of lose their luster as a person matures. To be honest, even the current crop of pirates doesn't interest me as much as they used to. But I can offer you a friendly piece of advice: if you have a family member you think appears destined to one day become a colorful branch on your own family tree, my suggestion is to keep it to yourself. And especially, don't tell *them* about your suspicions. The chances are, they won't appreciate your theory, and besides, they won't live to enjoy their true fame. Their pirate tendencies won't be fully appreciated until several generations have passed, anyway, so why get them all excited?

One For The Road—A Volleyball Trip

I've been a volleyball coach for many years, and in comparison to coaches in other sports, volleyball coaches usually enjoy an image of being relatively serene and well behaved. We typically don't throw chairs or storm the court and stand toe-to-toe with officials, casting aspersions on the heritage of their parentage. But that doesn't mean volleyball coaches don't worry, fret and fume, and road trips can be especially trying times for coaches. Over the years, I took many memorable road trips with my teams, but one trip in particular stands out.

I was coaching at a small high school, and we had always been at the bottom of the food chain in our conference. That year, however, we had a better-than-average team, judging by my preseason analysis. Four of our girls had actually seen a volleyball, and a fifth believed she had once held one in her hand. (To be fair, it was either a volleyball or a cantaloupe...she was pretty young at the time, and couldn't exactly remember—but her father was a minister, so I gave her the benefit of the doubt.)

With talent like that to work with, it's no wonder I was more optimistic about our chances that season than I had been in a long time. In preseason play, we soundly thrashed the junior high boys' wrestling squad, and we could regularly beat our JV team. Even more exciting was the fact that someone had reported actually having seen daylight beneath the sneakers of our center hitter when she went up for a block during a match with the all-star team from our local senior citizens center! (To be fair, I should confess that the seniors handed us our only loss during that preseason.)

With all that going for us, I was confident that this team had the potential to lift our school to new heights in our league—or at least get us out of the cellar. (Remember: I said I was excited, not crazy.) So I found myself looking forward to our first road trip of the season…something that I'd never felt before.

The afternoon of the trip, we boarded the team bus, full of optimism and excitement. I refer to it as the team bus, but its real name was "Baby Bunny," because it had a picture of a bunny painted on its side. Since it was a nothing-special, regular old school bus during the day, the bunny picture helped the kindergarten kids find the right bus in the afternoon. Somehow though, I just couldn't bring myself to strike my best coach's pose and shout, "Awright, everybody, listen up! Let's grab your gear and get on Baby Bunny!"

That night, as we bounced toward our destination, I could hear the girls buzzing with anticipation. It was good to know the team was focused. I leaned over in time to overhear Wendy say to Jennifer, "Hey, Jen, what did you get for the answer to question nine in the math quiz today?"

"I dunno. I had to skip it."

"Yeah, me, too."

I looked over at Raphael, my assistant coach, who was sitting in the seat across from me. I could tell he was deep in thought.

"Hey, Raph," I said. "Whatcha thinkin' 'bout? Our second rotation at middle blocker?"

"Huh? What?" he replied. "Sorry, coach. I musta dozed off."

Ah, it was going to be a magic night. I could just feel it. Soon I became involved in heavy thought myself—and was awakened when Baby Bunny rumbled into our opponent's parking lot.

As I walked through the double doors of the gym, I was immediately struck by several things that caused me concern. (Not that I need a whole lot of cause to whip myself into a frenzy. After all, worry has always been second nature to me. For instance, once, while I was in high school myself, I worried so much about an upcoming physics test that I couldn't eat or sleep for several days. It was only Mom's quick thinking that saved me from developing an ulcer. She reminded me that it was my sister's test and not mine, which relieved my anxiety considerably.)

The first thing that caught my eye in that shiny new gym was the school's vast array of banners. There wasn't enough room among the rafters to hold them all! The entire space overhead was a jumble of color, filled with banners of every size and description, proclaiming the wide variety of championships their various teams had won over the years. They covered every available inch of the rafters and walls. The place looked like the aftermath of an explosion in a trophy warehouse.

Our school's only banner hung from the rafters of our gym like a dead squid, feebly whispering, "State Finals, Girls Basketball, 1897." The banner didn't even say how we'd done, and though I hated to admit it, I assumed we'd lost. The faded lettering looked like it had been hand-cut with a pair of scissors by a fifth grader and was barely readable. But doggone it, it was our school's only claim to fame, and by golly, we cherished that old banner.

Just between you and I, that banner was also a clue to another little secret that nobody in our school ever talked about, which was that our school hadn't been officially incorporated until 1903. But we just figured that the records had somehow gotten garbled at some time in the distant past, and since there was no one still alive from that great old team to set the record straight, we took our banner's declaration as gospel. If the banner said that our school had once been in the State Finals, hey, that was good enough for us.

In all honesty, though, it really wasn't the tangled mass of banners overhead that bothered me most about that school's gym. Upon closer examination, I could swear that I could see other more ominous objects up there, as well—some of which looked suspiciously like shrunken heads! I told myself I must have been seeing things, especially since those shrunken heads were partially obscured by a number of what looked for all the world like scalps or hides, so I couldn't really get a good look at them.

I forced myself to turn my attention away from the rafters and toward the court. It was newly painted and incredibly shiny, but it seemed to be full of holes. Well, they weren't holes exactly. They looked more like small bomb craters. As I bent down to inspect them more closely, I could see the names of several popular brands of volleyballs imprinted into the wood at the bottom of each crater.

I looked up again, and this time, I knew that what I had taken for hides were actually the bleached white skins of dead volleyballs, deposited in the rafters following their explosion by a massive spike. To tell you the truth, it was hard to decide if that discovery made me feel better or worse.

Secretly, I began to worry, but I couldn't let the girls know that. I sent them to the locker room to suit up, and then walked over to our bench. While I waited, the home team came out to warm up. In turn, each player ran onto the floor, leaped over the net, and came down in a perfectly executed forward dive. (I may have been wrong about that, but that's how it appeared to me at the time, what with my mind reeling and all.)

Then the other team began to hit...*hard*. In fact, I had to cover my head with my clipboard to protect myself from flying shrapnel as volleyballs exploded everywhere around me. Thankfully, they'd run out of ammunition before my girls finally emerged from the locker room.

What happened the rest of that night is a little blurry. The only thing I really remember is that we arrived back home early that night. I'm sure the game was a disaster, just like most of our games that season. But in our team's defense, we did manage to hold our own with many other teams we faced that year—right up through the opening introductions—and that season turned out to be a fairly successful…at least by our school's standards.

Looking back on that trip now, I'm reminded of the words of a wise man who once described the human mind as the ultimate computer. Given the right commands, he said, our human computer is capable of recalling every incident of a person's life—the good, the bad, the victories, and the losses.

I don't know about you, but in my case, there are also times when I'm glad that my own computer is blessed with an "erase" button.

The Ramblin' Gary Show

I have to admit, I'm not much of a fisherman, but that hasn't stopped me from harboring a secret desire to have my own fishing show. You know, a show like those Saturday morning shows where the host reels in ten or fifteen big bass (using only one lure) in a half hour, without ever losing any line to snags or low-hanging trees.

Of course, my show would be totally different from those shows. My show would be designed to appeal to guys like me—guys who never catch fish. After all, that's one thing I'm really good at—not catching fish.

So you can get a feel for the premise, here's what a typical show would sound like:

"Hi, everybody! Welcome to the 'Ramblin' Gary Show.' Today, we're going in search of the elusive small mouth bass, but first, let's take a look at what we'll be using for tackle. Since bass are cantankerous and tend to hang out in snags and brush, we know we'll be losing quite a bit of line—I'm estimating about 72 miles worth. So I've rigged my reel with several brand-new skeins of line.

"For bait, I know a lot of those big time fishermen use lures with fancy names and huge price tags, but since I always lose my lures to snags and trees long before I catch any fish, we'll be using nothing but good ol' night crawlers, especially since I can't seem to get bites on anything else, anyway.

"I'll be solo paddling as we move around the lake today, with our cameraman filming from another canoe. He refuses to ride with me after last week, when I stood up while trying to land a fish, thus tipping us over and dumping $30,000 worth of gear into the river. I know, the guy's a crybaby, but whatcha gonna do?

"We're about ready to go, but before we push out into the water, here's a word from our sponsor, Fast Eddie's Worm Emporium."

(Fast Eddie would be a natural to sponsor my fishin' show, since he's the neighborhood kid who sells me my night crawlers. He always has a large stock of nice worms on hand, and leaves the light on in his bedroom at night so I can poke my head in his window and buy worms even after his parents have gone to bed. They really don't mind, especially since Eddie's already made enough money selling me worms to be able attend Harvard Medical School. Eddie also takes major credit cards, which is convenient, and holds the second mortgage on my house.)

"OK. We're back. The first thing you'll notice is that I'm now standing waist deep in the lake, since I accidentally tipped over my canoe while you were gone. So we'll be spending the next few minutes fishing around in the water for my pole and tackle box, which seem to have sunk to the bottom of the lake—which brings up a good point for all you beginners out there. It's a good idea to buy fishing gear that *floats*, in case of just such an emergency. I know that'll be the #1 thing on my list of equipment to add to my own tackle box—just as soon as I get Fast Eddie paid off, which won't be for about 26 years yet, since he gave a 30-year fixed rate. But for right now, until I can find my pole we're kind of at a loss as to what to do next. So maybe we should take another short break, this time for the American Worm Ranchers Association."

(You see? Being a dedicated worm fisherman, I've given this fishin' show idea quite a bit of thought.)

"Welcome back. You'll notice that my line is now tangled in that low-hanging branch over there, causing my worm to dangle about six inches above the waterline. I know that may seem strange to many of you, but I'm doing it to illustrate a point. After all, any darned fool can catch fish by simply tossing a worm into the water. But it takes a *real* fisherman to catch a fish with his worm suspended above the waterline! As a true sportsman, I believe in always trying to make the contest between man and beast as even as possible.

"Come to think of it, that brings up another point that I'd like to clear up. I want it known, here and now, that I was into 'catch and release' *years* before that practice became fashionable, yet I've never gotten any credit for it. I guess the problem was that since I never caught any fish, I never actually got a chance to release any. But I'm telling you, if I would ever would've caught any fish, I would've released them, I swear! As far as I can see, the whole thing is just a matter of semantics, if you think about it."

(At this point, the show would another break, this time for artificial worms, which, I must admit, have never worked for me, but still seems like a logical sponsor for a fishin' show like mine.)

"OK, we're back again. Unfortunately, I know none of you can see me right now, since our cameraman dozed off and fell into the river just before we came back on the air. Of course, you know what that means—I'm going to have to listen to the guy whine all afternoon about a bunch more ruined equipment—like it was my fault or something!

"Well, that's about all the time we have for this week, but I hope you'll join me next time, when we'll be going after one of the biggest and most challenging game fish of all—the majestic marlin. Of course, since we live 2000 miles away from the nearest body of water that might actually *contain* a marlin, our chances of *catching* a marlin are fairly slim. But that's the great thing about a show like this. Since we never catch any fish on this show anyway, we can *say* we're fishing for whatever we want, right? So we might as well go after something really big!

"So till we meet again, I'll say what I say every week…keep trying. Who knows, maybe someday we'll actually catch something—anything would be good."

Ahhh…I can see it now. 'The Ramblin' Gary Show.'

Hey, it's not impossible. After all, it's entirely possible that there's been an audience of frustrated anglers out there who are just like me, and they've been waiting for the day that someone would produce a fishing show they could relate to—one geared toward guys just like them. Guys who can fish all day without a bite, regardless of whether it's for crappies, bass, catfish—or marlin.

You never know…it could happen.

Small-time Halftimes Are Big-time By Me

When I first moved to rural Iowa, one of the things that intrigued me most was the halftime at our local high school football games. I can still remember the first one I witnessed. As the teams left the field, I looked around and wondered what had happened to our cheerleaders. I couldn't blame them if they'd taken that moment to race indoors and try to warm up their poor frozen little pompons.

But that wasn't the case. Moments later, our high school band came marching out onto the field, and I soon realized that all our cheerleaders but one had been pressed into service, either as members of the band or the flag team. (I admit, jaded person that I can sometimes be, I couldn't help wondering how that one lone cheerleader had managed to escape being drafted.)

But there were other unique aspects of my first halftime show. In the middle of the pack, I saw our home team's number 77, now taking the field as a different kind of lineman, tackling a tuba this time, marching in his blue jersey and black cleats. He was followed by our team mascot, dressed in full uniform, banging on the cymbals.

It was an amazing menagerie, dressed more like refugees from a Goodwill clearance sale than a high school marching band. But those of us who watched them offered our full support and we loved them all the more for their efforts. It was my initiation into small-time halftimes, and a spectacle I will never forget.

Without warning, a screaming gust of wind whipped across the field, briefly lifting the jersey-wearing tuba player into the air. Whatever tune the band was playing at that moment (I couldn't tell what it was) was graced with at least one surprise bass note as our poor tackle suddenly became airborne. To his credit, he made a sincere attempt to keep marching, his feet suspended in midair.

The frigid wind was biting hard that night, and as our majorette went to fling her baton into the air, the metal stuck to her sweaty palm. She grimaced in pain, but went on with her routine as best she could, considering she now had a two-foot piece of pipe glued to the skin of her right hand.

The music menagerie flailed away, tackling tune after tune, some recognizable only because the public address announcer had told us what they were supposed to be before the band began playing. Finally, to the ragged beat of several numb-handed drummers, our band lumbered off the field to the muffled applause from fifty pairs of gloved hands.

But I loved every second of it. In my mind, it represented the true spirit of what our country is all about. It was our small town version of Do-It-Yourself High Art, and showed what extraordinary steps we would take, by golly, to have a halftime show! Ragged or not, those smalltime halftime shows seemed like Big Time to us. After all, this is *America*, and make no mistake, we *do* it—in spite all odds.

Old Dogs Dye Hard

It all started with my kids, really. They went through a phase where it became very important to dye their hair various colors, so being a good dad, I offered to help them. We had just gotten my daughter the nicest shade of violet, and were beginning to work on helping my son achieve a two-tone black-and-white color scheme, when my son said, "Hey, Dad. Why don't you do your hair?"

I started to explain that guys didn't dye their hair, but then I realized how silly that would sound, since I was in the process of putting dye on the top of his head at that very moment, so I said, "Hmm…I dunno."

Then I changed my mind and decided, why not? But since I had no experience with it, I was nervous. I've always had the uncanny ability to take a difficult situation and turn it into an unmitigated disaster, and this seemed like a candidate for just that type of scenario. After all, I wasn't interested in purple hair—I had something more akin to simply covering some of the grey in mind.

Still, I thought, it might be fun to try something new, so I said, "OK, I'll do it!"

So the next day found me at the local department store, walking as casually as I could down an aisle filled with hair dye, trying to make sense of the baffling array of products available. It was quite an eye-opener. There were hundreds of colors and brands, all marked with what seemed to be secret codes on them—codes that apparently were only decipherable by folks who dyed their hair on a regular basis.

Some of the displays actually had locks of hair attached to the front of the shelf, designed, I supposed, to let would-be customers know what their hair would look like after they'd treated it with that particular shade. The trouble was, the locks weren't large enough to really be able to tell what a whole head of hair would look like after using that color.

I looked at the boxes, which all featured pictures of women. I had to train my eye to look at the actual hair color being pictured, and not get distracted by the hairstyle or length of hair worn by the model on the box. The whole process was made more difficult by the fact that I had to pretend to be looking at something else every time a woman came down the aisle and began looking for her own favorite shade. I decided that if anyone asked me, I would tell them I was looking for dye for my wife, even though I didn't even have a wife at that time. I figured it was only small fib, one that probably wouldn't go too hard on me come Judgment Day.

I finally found a hair color that looked really nice on the very attractive model pictured on the box. Her hair was long and golden, and reminded me of the surfer hair I had always dreamed of having when I was a kid and worshipped the music of the Beach Boys. (Never mind that we lived 2000 miles from the nearest body of water in which a person actually could surf. I was a closet surfer, and I figured that if I couldn't surf in reality, I could at least look like a surfer.)

I picked up the dye and walked to the checkout counter, feeling as nervous as a bootlegger trying to sneak moonshine past a border guard. But I felt better; knowing I had my, "It's for my wife" excuse to fall back on, just in case someone started asking questions. To my surprise, the clerk didn't even up. She just rang up the dye and handed me my sack. I slunk out of the store, still feeling as if the Dye Police would come racing after me any moment and bust me on the way to my truck. But I made it home, and prepared "to do the deed," as William Shakespeare had once said on the day he first decided to touch up his own hair.

The instructions on the package were only slightly less understandable than your average ancient Sanskrit tablet, so I tossed them aside and began slopping the mixture on top of my head. It seemed easy enough, I reasoned: just lather the stuff in, let it sit for who-knows-how-long, rinse it out, and viola, instant surfer hair!

I let the dye sit on my scalp for an hour or so. By that time, my hair had dried to the consistency of cement, so I figured it was probably time to rinse the stuff out. I have to tell you, I was excited—and more than a little nervous. As I stepped into the shower, I caught a glimpse of myself in the mirror, and it seemed like there was a little more red highlight in my hair than I'd expected.

When I stepped out of the shower and looked in the mirror, I was shocked. My hair was bright red! I looked like Lucy Ricardo on her worst hair day ever. Oh my, what had I done? I couldn't go out looking like this. I'd wanted golden surfer hair, and I was now wearing what looked to be a very cheap clown wig on my head!

I had to do something—fast! So I got dressed and ran out the door. On my way to my truck, several butterflies tried to land on my head, apparently mistaking me for a geranium. An angry redheaded woodpecker buzzed me, protecting his territory from what he must have thought was an unwelcome intruder.

I drove to a different store this time, hoping I wouldn't run into anyone I knew. I had a cowboy hat shoved down as far as it would go on my head. I wore dark glasses, and pulled my collar up around my ears. I looked like a refuge from the Dalton Gang, casing a bank for future reference. As I slunk into the store, I had no doubt that every security camera was instantly trained on me, since I'm guessing they get very few customers who look as suspicious as I did that morning.

But I didn't care. I headed straight for the hair dye section; glad it was in the back of the store. But what was I going to do? Should I try to find an "anti-red" dye to cover my Fire Engine #9? I wasn't sure. I just stood there for a long time, nearly paralyzed with fear and feeling an ever-growing sense of despair beginning to wash over me. But I *had* to do something. I wasn't about to have to endure a lifetime of Woody Woodpecker jokes from the folks around town. After all, jokes in a small town can have a LONG shelf life.

Sometimes, though, in the midst of your greatest despair, fate steps in with the helping hand you need. As I stood in the aisle, fighting back tears or remorse and regret, a kindly little old lady walked up to me. Without the slightest hesitation, she said softly, "Get the wrong color, didja, young fella?"

I looked at her and shook my head. Then, without knowing why, I took off my cowboy hat and let her see my flaming red locks. She didn't laugh, but she was clearly shocked.

She said, "That's quite a hairdo, young man, but I think you'd do better with an ash."

At first, I was a little offended by that. Ash? What was she saying? Set my hair on fire and then live with the residue? I knew the situation was bad, but I didn't think I'd end up having to use a slash-and-burn technique to fix it.

She saw my puzzled expression and said, "No, no. I mean, an ash-based color. Look here…" she picked up a box and showed me a color that was marked "Medium Ash Blonde."

"Your hair color needs to stay within the ash family of colors, or the results might be, shall we say—unpredictable."

I said, "Shall we say catastrophic."

She nodded in agreement. "Sonny, would you mind putting your hat back on? The glare off your hair is starting to give me a migraine."

"Oh, sorry," I said, forgetting I'd taken the hat off. I jammed it back on before anyone could come by and see me wearing a fire hydrant on the top of my head.

"If you use this Medium Ash Blonde, I think you'll be much happier with the results," she said, handing the box to me. "Of course, since you're going to be mixing it with that red you've already got, I'm not quite sure what might happen."

I thanked her, telling her that almost any color would be an improvement over the one I had now, and she agreed, saying, "I think you're right about that, young man. Well, good luck. And by the way, if I were you, I'd keep my hat on till I got home. You wouldn't want anyone to mistake you for an accident victim and try to tie a tourniquet around your head."

I went up to the counter, followed by at least a half dozen undercover store detectives, to pay for my life-saving ash product. To my chagrin, the clerk looked at it, then bent over and called into the microphone by her register, "Can I get a price check on Medium Ash Blonde hair color, please?"

Everyone in all the other aisles seemed to look up at the same time, and straight at me—the guy with the flaming red hair. I pulled up my collar and croaked, "It's...it's for my wife..."

I felt like I'd just been caught trying to sneak ten pounds of heroin into a maximum-security prison. My voice cracked. I said some more things, but in a language that didn't sound like English. I was sure the whole store was echoing to the sound of my knees knocking. But I stayed put, determined to walk out of the store with a product that might help regain my natural hair color again, although at that moment, I wouldn't have been able to swear in court as to what that color actually was—it seemed like such a long time since I'd seen it.

I paid the lady, slunk back out to my truck, and sped home. I had only one thought in mind: I needed to get this ash on head and get on with my life! And yet, something kept nagging at me. Who in their right mind would put ashes on their head? After all, I'd heard of "dishwater blonde," but it was always used as a derogatory term. But the more I thought about it, the more appeal dumping dishwater on my head seemed to have, compared to smearing it with ashes! Then I had a brainstorm. (The kind of brainstorm only a man could have.) I could do a test run for free, before I made another mistake and had to parade around with hair the color of who-knows-what burned-out building.

When I got into the house, I went downstairs to our wood-burning furnace. I opened the door and stuck my head inside. Good! There were lots of ashes in there! And flames. I forgot about the flames. Now my hair was not only red, but was smoking! I looked like a human stick of incense!

I must admit, though, it did give me a rosy complexion—all the way down to my chest hair! But the smell was pretty overwhelming, and as I ran upstairs to hose myself down, I set off our smoke alarms, and the overhead sprinklers came on.

Things started to go downhill from there. Water poured from the ceiling, drenching our wall-to-wall carpets, and for the rest of that winter, I had to wear black rubber boots while I waited for that carpet to dry out. That wasn't so bad, but those boots looked a little funny with my pajamas, and they left black marks all over the hardwood floor in my kitchen.

Eventually, I had to admit that rubbing ashes on my head turned out to be one of my more bone-headed stunts—and for me, that's saying something!

I sucked up my courage and applied my hard-won ash-colored hair dye, and to my sweet surprise, it worked! The red disappeared, and my hair again looked relatively natural. But that was the good news. The bad news was that I now had to live with the realization that every time someone asked me what color my hair was, I'd have to tell them it was ash-colored. From that day forward, I could never aspire to having the kind of silky, shiny hair I saw in television commercials. I mean, how many shiny piles of ashes have you seen in your lifetime?

Ah, but sometimes the truth hurts...and sets your chest on fire...and triggers smoke alarms...and leaves black marks on the kitchen floor.

Grandpa's Knife

"Charge any common thing with the high voltage of understanding and emotion and you have the materials for a work of art."

—David Grayson

Sometimes, when I'm feeling stressed or feel the need to refocus, I find myself thinking about my grandpa's knife. Some folks drink or take pills in an attempt to manage stress. Some folks handle their rosary beads. But my grandpa whittled.

My brothers and I could always tell when there was something weighing on Grandpa's mind. He'd pick up several short sticks, sit on the porch swing, and begin to whittle. We could judge the size of the problem he was grappling with by the size of the pile of shavings at the old man's feet.

As far as I knew, Grandpa never whittled anything useful, but that was never his purpose. He just took any old stick and began whittling it into a point. Then, he'd keep whittling until the stick was too short for him to hold, at which time he'd set it down and start on another one. I marveled at his ability to focus so intensely, just sitting there, gently rocking the porch swing, quietly whittling his problem down to size. Then, guided by some inner signal known only to him, we'd see Grandpa suddenly stand up, and we knew he'd reached a conclusion. He picked up a small whiskbroom that always stood beside the swing, cleaned up the shavings, and walked away in silence.

There were also times when Grandpa's knife helped teach us other lessons—lessons that were more difficult to face. No matter what our indiscretion had been, we boys knew there would come a time after we'd received our punishment when Grandpa would call us to come and sit on the porch steps. Holding several sticks in his left hand, he'd reach into his overalls with his right hand and pull out his old knife. Then he'd sit on the swing and begin to whittle, slowly and deliberately, never looking at us, not saying a word.

After what seemed a very long time, he'd finally begin to talk, softly but firmly, about whatever it was that we had done, why it was wrong, and how disappointed he was that we were having to have this little talk. All the while, thin slivers of wood gently floated to the floor as his knife deftly cut into the stick he was whittling.

By keeping his eyes fixed on his whittling, Grandpa made certain he never saw the tears rolling down our faces as the consequences of our actions slowly washed over us. He never tried to drive home any big point. He always spoke in gentle tones, and when he was finished, he'd stand, snap his old knife shut, put it back in his pocket, and turn to walk away, never quite looking at us directly.

"Clean up those shavings, will you, boys?" he'd say as he slowly walked off the porch. The lesson had been learned, and there was nothing left to say.

You know, it's kind of sad in a way. People don't seem to whittle the way they used to, at least not the way Grandpa used to, or for the same reasons. I don't even carry a knife, and neither do most folks I know. But there are times when I'm working at the lathe in my shop when a long piece of wood will curl up from the knife and float to the floor. Then I'm suddenly eight years old again, watching my grandpa sitting on the porch swing, quietly whittling.

At those times, I reach down, pick up the shaving and watch it curl around my finger. Then I just stand for a long moment, remembering, until a thought crosses my mind. Maybe I *will* get myself a small pocketknife, after all. You never can tell when the urge to whittle might overtake me.

About the Author

Gary Anderson has been a freelance writer for more than twenty years, but only got "serious" about his writing after he moved to rural Iowa with his two children, Casey Rose and Cody. Since his arrival in the Hawkeye State, Gary has sold articles to more than a dozen magazines, published two books of his own, and has had stories also appear in several other anthologies. Since 1996, he has written the "Wit and Wisdom" column for *Iowa REC News*. Many of the stories contained in *Spider's Big Catch* first appeared in that column.

He has also edited several monthly publications over the years, as well as a number of full-length manuscripts for various publishing houses in the United States and Canada. He still performs as a musician, playing churches and the occasional club, as well as giving motivational presentations to various gatherings, during which, as he says, "I play a few songs, tell a few tall tales, and read from my books."

Gary divides his time between his home in western Oregon with his wife Tiffany and daughters Brittney and Tori, and on his small farm perched on the banks the Turkey River in northeastern Iowa with his daughter, Casey Rose, and son, Cody. On his Iowa farm, he says, "I can't see my nearest neighbor, there's no traffic and I'm forced to spend much of his day watching deer and wild turkeys wander across the fields while I'm working in my studio. I know—it's a tough job, but somebody's gotta do it."

Gary's first collection of short stories, *Spider's Night on the Boom*, was published in 2001. If you'd like to touch bases with Gary, his email address is abciowa@hotmail.com.

0-595-23443-7